T0209303

PEACE IN ALGIERS

JAN HENDRIX

PEACE IN ALGIERS

iUniverse books may be ordered through booksellers or by contacting:

iUniverse
1663 Liberty Drive
Bloomington, IN 47403
www.iuniverse.com
844-349-9409

Because of the dynamic nature of the Internet, any web addresses or links contained in this book may have changed since publication and may no longer be valid. The views expressed in this work are solely those of the author and do not necessarily reflect the views of the publisher, and the publisher hereby disclaims any responsibility for them.

Any people depicted in stock imagery provided by Getty Images are models, and such images are being used for illustrative purposes only. Certain stock imagery © Getty Images.

ISBN: 978-1-6632-4376-8 (sc)
ISBN: 978-1-6632-4377-5 (e)

Library of Congress Control Number: 2022914984

Print information available on the last page.

iUniverse rev. date: 08/30/2022

CONTENTS

CHAPTER 1

PEACE

Algiers 1962

By 1961 the plan to keep Algiers under France's rule was becoming a hopeless situation for the Algiers Europeans, the army, and especially the Paris government. Many had been killed on all sides, including numerous innocent civilians. Because of the countless factions, there didn't seem to be a solution that would appease the FLN— the National Liberation Front, the main force against France rule. They demanded total independence. A radical faction of the FLN fought on, unconcerned with the cost to human life. De Gaulle saw the hopelessness of the war and was openly considering complete independence. The Europeans in Algiers—*Pied-Noirs,* as they were called, many in the army—were in direct disagreement with his plans.

De Gaulle and most of his Paris government decided the war was too costly and hopeless and wanted to stop it by granting independence to the Algerian rebels. Some in France and most of the Europeans in Algiers did not agree and wanted the French army to remain in the country. Although the Europeans numbered closed to a million and had lived and built businesses and homes there, they knew if they came under the rule of the FLN—which numbered about fifty million—they and their families would suffer. But they could not exist without the French army. This was a no-win situation for the French and other Europeans living in Algiers.

Colonel Devon realized this and made it known that although he disagreed with Paris's decision, he served in the French army and had to go along with the Paris government. Immediately after he made his decision he called an emergency meeting of his entire command.

He announced, "We have new orders. Now we're to focus on our people queuing up at the ports and help them through this terrible ordeal of relocating. We'll certainly obey these orders. But we're also ordered to ignore the general population. This means we're no longer to protect those friendly Muslims who have stayed peaceful, as well as those who helped us in our fight."

He paused and looked around, obviously judging their reaction. Low grunts of dissatisfaction arose from his staff before him.

"But my personal intention is to protect all that we can, in spite of Paris." He paused again as words of agreement came from the staff.

After taking a drag on his cigarette and exhaling a cloud of white smoke upward, he continued. "I'm setting up teams to mingle in the crowds at the ports and make sure no one mistreats or harm them in any way. Since most of our army will be recalled back to France and can't support us, we're shorthanded. Therefore, I will be one of the team members, along with Lieutenant Adelle and Sergeant Boivin."

Adelle and Boivin nodded in agreement but remained silent.

"We'll began our patrols early tomorrow morning. Let's all do our jobs well and help our people waiting to be shipped out at the ports."

The following morning, as the colonel and his team approached the loading docks, they were shocked at the sight of the crowd awaiting evacuation. Thousands of Europeans, mostly French, stood unprotected, waiting. No breeze existed and the humidity was high. The sky was clear of clouds and the sun bore down, bringing early morning heat. Most of the people looked confused, lost, and unhappy. They stood around in family groups, huddled for protection. Able to bring only a single suitcase with them, many stooped over their open suitcases to retrieve hats and umbrellas to protect them from the coming heat of the day, which would soon be upon them. Men gathered around their families to help protect them from the press of the crowds. Women stood next to the men with arms outstretched to keep their children from wandering away from their small, protected area. Some women held babies in their arms and leaned against their men.

A few soldiers were mixed in the crowds, alert and ready to help the citizens.

The colonel approached one soldier, who stiffened up and saluted.

"At ease, soldier," he said quietly, returning the salute. "What can you tell me of the situation here?"

"Sir," the soldier began. "It's a sad sight, seeing our people forced from their homes where they had built businesses, schools, and communities and lived for generations to be forced to leave it all. I want to help but there's so many; what can I do?"

"Just try to protect them and keep order the best you can. I'll be mingling with the crowds throughout the day and will check with you as often as I can."

Lieutenant Adelle and Sergeant Boivin were with the colonel. Standing on either side of him, each carrying a MAS-38 submachine gun in addition to their side arms, they looked formidable and in charge. Although the heavy guns couldn't be used because of ricochets bouncing around in the crowds, they were carried to show the army was in charge and to keep terrorists at bay. In case of trouble, if weapons were needed, they were ordered by the colonel to use only their sidearms. The soldier waited before the colonel, saluting again. Having an officer around would relieve him of much responsibility.

The colonel had the lieutenant and sergeant with him because he was on the FLN's assassination list. Knowing how effective the terrorists were, General Chalet had ordered the two to be with the colonel whenever he was in public.

The two soldiers were exceptional. Lieutenant Adelle was well known and respected. From the beginning, Bernadette Adelle was a standout in all aspects of her army career. She had an amazing perception of military situations and history. She had intelligent opinions of how and why certain battle were lost and others won. Not only did she perform admirably in all aspects of her military training, she fired at expert level with the service pistol at close distances and far. She could draw and shoot with a speed that astounded her training instructors. She didn't have to aim but simply picked the spot on her target and let her instincts do the rest. It didn't take her superiors long to realize she was officer material, and they promoted her to the rank of lieutenant.

After serving in Algiers for a time, she was assigned to a special intelligent detachment under Colonel Devon, a highly respected officer who had seen much combat. It was a special detachment that was organized specifically to confront terrorists, and it was extremely efficient. The lieutenant had seen combat also; while on an assignment, and monitoring a parade, she was confronted by a terrorist wandering through the crowds, shooting indiscriminately. Caught off guard, she was shot twice, once in her side and another in her left leg. While falling to the ground, she drew her service pistol and fired two rounds that brought the terrorist down with well-placed lethal shots. This brought her fame with the other soldiers and she became highly respected. Although she was uncomfortable with the fame, and felt a little guilty about it, knowing other soldiers had done as much. And being an attractive female soldier, she already had more attention than she wanted. She wanted to stay strictly military, and she took seriously her bodyguard role with the colonel.

Colonel Devon thought highly of her and praised her often. Sometimes the lieutenant felt he was praising and watching her more than necessary. At first, she felt good about being noticed so often, but eventually she became concerned when she realized when their eyes met, she held the look, as well. *Hold on, soldier,* she told herself. *Just settle down. You know there can be no emotional contact between the commander and someone in his command.* It was strictly forbidden by high command, and she was absolutely not going to risk her hard-won military reputation for anybody.

The colonel and team moved through the crowds, speaking encouragement and offering sympathy. Both the lieutenant and sergeant hovered close to him, their attention covering his movements. One watched for activity in the rear, while the other guarded the front. With a signal, they sometimes switched up their observations.

A large troop ship stationed at the port slowly loaded passengers. Soldiers were stationed at the loading ramp to keep order and assist some of the helpless ones. Another ship waited in the distance to move in as soon as the current ship was loaded and headed back to a European port.

The next day was the same, with Lieutenant Adelle and Sergeant Boivin closely following Colonel Devon. In spite of being strictly military and familiar with the war situation, by the flowering day, Adelle was becoming disturbed with so many people in such distress. She was subconsciously shifting her attitude and attention from a firm military one to that of sympathy for the displaced citizens; she wanted to help. She got permission from the colonel to help some of the women with children. The colonel thought this was a good idea and took her MAS-38 submachine gun to give her more freedom to help.

Adelle approached a woman holding a crying baby with another little one crying at her feet. She asked the lady if she could help and picked up the one on the ground, attempting to console it. The child stopped crying and nestled up to Adelle. Adelle held the child close, cooing and whispering softly. The child hugged Adelle, and with this love and warmth, for the first time began to lessen her military mind-set and felt a special feeling she was unaccustomed to. From somewhere deep in her instincts a femininity emerged, giving her a good feeling. The child fell asleep, and Adelle lay her gently next to the lady now sitting in the grass holding the baby.

The lady looked up, giving Lieutenant Adelle a special thank you nod. Adelle nodded back, displaying sincere sympathy and understanding.

"I must move on, but if you need me, I'll be close," she told the woman. The woman tried to speak but choked up with gratitude.

The days were long and hot as the colonel's team worked their way through the crowds, helping and encouraging. There were a million Europeans in Algiers, and almost all wanted to leave before the army moved out and the FLN took over. The Paris Agreement had stated the army would not interfere with the FLN as they took over the businesses and homes of the departing Europeans. The colonel scoffed at this command, saying his detachment would continue to protect the people the same as before, and if the radicals got in the way, too bad for them.

CHAPTER 2

LIEUTENANT ADELLE

Lieutenant Adelle agreed with the colonel to protect all, and if the FLN got in the way she'd deal with them, the same as before the Peace Agreement. But after several days of helping the people crowded at the docks, she developed a new attitude about the war. It was sad seeing people lose their life savings and homes they had built over generations.

At day's end she returned to her quarters and compared notes with her roommate, Lieutenant Jennie. It took two glasses of wine with their army chow for each to come down sufficiently to shower and crash in their individual beds. But although she was exhausted, she had trouble falling asleep. Remembering the crying faces of the children as she picked them up and cuddled them, and the way they clung to her after they quieted down and she had to move on. This was a new experience for her, helping people with care and attention and not a gun.

She was already struggling with the emotional impact of her growing feelings for the colonel, and the two sensitive issues kept her confused and upset. The matter with the colonel was a no-hope situation, for she in no way would violate the strict rule of commander- personnel separation. It would simply look like she was using sex to gain favors from her commander. The other soldiers would look down on her, and she could not stand for this. She was now held in high regard, and she simply stood too proud to destroy that reputation.

Making the situation more difficult was the belief Colonel Devon had strong feelings for her. When she was on watch with Sergeant Boivin, the colonel sat at a distance from her, but sometimes when their eyes met, it was hard for them to turn away. She wanted to stay at a distance, but her bodyguard assignment kept her close. She thought about conferring with the army chaplain to get help with reassignment but knew this wouldn't work; it would reveal their situation and she was not going to let that happen. The best she could do was stay busy, keeping her distracted.

Unfortunately, her situation got worse. After three days of pushing and shoving through the crowds, helping when needed and passing along encouragement, the colonel announced at the end of day the three of them needed a break and should have dinner at his favorite café, the colonel's treat.

But halfway through the dinner, Colonel Devon called Sergeant Boivin over and told him his desk sergeant had asked for help arranging paperwork the general needed. Boivin finished his meal quickly and, nodding to Adelle, headed to headquarters.

She sat quietly eating a tuna sandwich and a small salad. She scanned the café patrons. When she looked in the colonel's direction, she caught him looking at her. She smiled and nodded a salute, and he chuckled and returned a subtle thumb's up. When his attention turned back to his lunch, she continued to look at him. For the first time, she realized she had feelings that went deeper than admiration. These emotions were something she had never felt for anyone before and they left her uncomfortable.

The colonel asked Adelle to sit at his table, an unusual request. Adelle was surprised and instantly on guard. As soon as she joined him at his table, he motioned for the waiter and ordered a bottle of expensive white wine.

Adelle was even more on guard. "What's the occasion, sir?"

"Just a small celebration after three days of hard work, Adelle." He smiled at her as he took a sip. "I want to congratulate you on your fine work with the refugees."

"Just doing what was necessary," she said, not touching her glass.

"We've got more work to do there, "he continued. "I'm saddened to see our people dislocated like this after they worked so hard to establish the communities. But that's war. It'll take many days to get all the people shipped out. Anyway, let's try to stay in good spirits; it's necessary to do our jobs." He tipped his glass, saying, "Cheers."

Adelle took a small sip from her glass, not looking at the colonel. She was becoming uncomfortable with the situation and tried to think of some way to avoid his looks.

After a short pause, the colonel said, "OK, Adelle, I'll get right to the point of this celebration. I want you to know I highly respect you and hold you in high regard, and I have strong feelings for you."

Adelle didn't know how to respond. She only looked down at her glass. After she had worked so hard at suppressing her feelings and finally had this under control, here he was making everything worse. She didn't speak, only fumbled with her glass, not drinking.

"This has been on my mind for some time and I want it out in the open." He paused again, then continued, looking closely at her. "I'd like to get together with you sometime, Adelle."

"Stop! Stop!" Adelle said. "Please don't say anymore. It can't happen! It won't happen!"

The colonel, seeing Adelle upset and not understanding her reaction, grew quiet for a moment. "I'm sorry I've upset you. I should have known it was too soon to mention this. Forgive me." He stood up. "Let's carry on as usual."

Adelle followed him without speaking. Although she was relieved to be returning to quarters, the situation weighed heavily on her consciousness. She had always been military-oriented, and now her disposition and comfort were taking on an entirely different character: she was recognizing her feminine nature and not just that of a soldier, and it made her uncomfortable.

Hold on, Lieutenant, she told herself. *This won't work. Cool off.* She focused on her lunch and observed the activity in the café without letting him see her looking his way. Still, she was more than a little surprised with her new awareness. Although the feeling was strange and unbidden in her mind, it brought a pleasant sensation to dwell on.

Her new experience with her femininity worried her to the point she needed someone to talk to about it. That evening back in her quarters with Lieutenant Jenney, she brought it up. After they had their two glasses of wine and the small talk ebbed, she said, "I have something to talk about that's got me worried."

"Out with it. I'm all ears."

"Well, it's something I hate to talk about. It's about my duty as a soldier and being the colonel's bodyguard."

"Umm—spill it!"

"Well, I've always been so on guard with everything military that nothing else bothered me." Adelle paused a moment, looking down as if trying to think of what to say.

Finally, she looked up and said, "I'm finding myself thinking more about the people and helping them … and having less of a military mind." She paused again. "It's just not a good way for a soldier to think."

"No, it's not. We've always got to be on guard. But the fact you realize it means you can control it."

"Yeah, my concern for the crying babies and distraught moms— I'm not afraid of that."

"So what's the big deal?"

"The big deal" She paused again, not saying anything for a few moments.

"Come on, out with it. You'll feel better afterward."

"I have feelings for the colonel," she blurted out. "And I can't help it!"

Lieutenant Jenny was silent for a time, staring at Adelle. Then: "OK, you do have a problem. That situation won't work. You can't have a relationship with your superior officer. It's strictly against the rules, and the others soldiers will ridicule you unmercifully for using sex to get special favors."

"I know, Jenny, I'm fighting it. I'm staying away from him as much as I can."

"It may help you to know, it's a known psychological fact that when you take care of something, you become emotionally attached to it. You're his bodyguard, and that's your hook." The lieutenant reached over and squeezed Adelle's arm in support. "Knowing this, you can fight it and get over it."

"I definitely will get over it, Jenny. Thanks for your help."

CHAPTER 3

SERGEANT BOIVIN

When the intelligent detachment analyst learned Colonel Devon was set for assassination by the FLN radicals, the general ordered an immediate protection detail for him. His orders stated that two of the best soldiers in the colonel's command be assigned exclusively to this detail. Lieutenant Adelle and Sergeant Boivin were considered the best and were ordered to provide that security. Lieutenant Adelle, the officer in charge, was ordered to make certain they stayed focused on the colonel. An attack could come at any time and from any direction.

Adelle had worked with Boivin on several assignments and trusted him, but she noticed he sometimes seemed preoccupied. She didn't know if it was the assignment or something else. But she knew he must be alert to the protection role, or he might let something important get by; in some cases that could be fatal. During their conversations he wouldn't bring up the subject. When she brought it up, he was silent and distant. She knew something was bothering him, but he needed to always be thinking of protecting the colonel. She was responsible for the assignment and knew they both must be focused in order to provide the needed protection. With this in mind she decided to question him, and they met at the local café for a beer.

Sergeant Boivin was glad to meet Adelle at the café. It was busy, but as they walked in a couple sitting at a streetside table got up and left. They took the table and then ordered two beers. The beer were frosty and cool, and each savored their first sip.

"Good ... umm," the lieutenant said, trying to get a conversation started.

Boivin nodded as he took a long sip but said nothing.

Adelle waited a moment. "This assignment will keep us busy, and we must stay very alert when the colonel is out of his office."

"Mm-hmm," was Boivin's only response.

Adelle decided to push the issue. "OK, Sergeant. You don't seem interested in the assignment. Why not?"

"The assignment is OK and I'll do my part. Besides, I'm under orders."

"Yes, you're under orders. You have no choice."

"I said I'd do my part, Lieutenant."

"OK, Sergeant, I'm glad you're with me on this. "Adelle looked at him closely. "But if you're not one hundred percent, I'll request another partner."

"I'm on it, Lieutenant!"

"Good," Adelle said, but she didn't feel confident about the situation.

The morning of the fourth day, Colonel Devon called a meeting before they were to leave for the ports. "OK, listen up, troops," he began. "It has come to my attention that some of the people waiting to be shipped out have run out of food. Not only are they suffering from being forced to leave, but they're stuck out in the open, waiting. And now this food problem. I lay awake last night trying to come up with a plan. We're don't have the resources to feed them, but I think I've got something that'll help out."

He paused for a moment, looking around, waiting to make sure he had everyone's attention. "I want us to approach a few friendly Muslim store owners to set up shop in the midst of the crowds to sell food and water. The people are not so poor to not have some funds to support themselves through the evacuation and after. With shops in their midst, it should help them as well as the shop owners."

"But, sir," Lieutenant Jennie said. "The radicals hate the Europeans and won't like the shop owners helping them. They'll make trouble for the shop owners."

"I know and in spite of the Paris Treaty that states our army is not to interfere with the FLN, we'll closely watch the shop owners as they work. If any FLN member gives the owners trouble, we'll step in."

A mummer of agreement broke out among the troops. Some of the soldiers had fought and lost friends to the brutal terrorists and welcomed a face-to-face confrontation.

A couple of the female soldiers were instructed to approach select shop owners with the colonel's idea. It went over well, for the opportunity to set up a food stand in the midst of the crowds would be profitable. Several owners set up shop right away.

At the ports, the colonel set up patrols to move through the crowds, helping out and keeping order. He, along with Lieutenant Adelle and Sergeant Boivin, patrolled through the waiting citizens. Dressed in camo fatigues with wide web belts that held their service weapons plus spare clips and accessories, they stood out in the crowds. Many watched them with nods of appreciation.

Adelle remained quiet as they walked along. She was becoming more affected by the pitiful looks and frightened faces as she moved through the crowd. When confronting a family with several children, some babies crying, she reached down and picked up the crying baby, cuddling it closely while the mother gave her a painful look of appreciation. Although both the colonel and the sergeant had sympathy for the displaced people, they knew Adelle's attention to the families could be more effective than theirs. Knowing this, the men patiently waited a short distance ahead, talking encouragingly to those in the crowd.

Seeing so much sadness, Adelle's mental state was becoming more and more sympathetic to the people's needs and less to military needs. Realizing this, she fought against her changing attitude, telling herself she was a lieutenant with an army at war and must stay on guard at all times. Her life and others' depended on a strict awareness of the situations she encountered. She blamed her growing emotional softness not just on the people queued up at the ports but on the colonel and his attempts to tell her his feelings. She also had feelings but didn't understand and struggled to suppress them.

Damn him! She told herself. He's just adding to my troubles. It's keeping me from the military mind-set that I need. At times she thought she hated him for bringing her so much worry.

She also was troubled with the thought she was unpolite when she didn't respond when he spoke of his feelings. She wished she had handled that situation better. This dichotomy of attitude versus reality weighed heavily on her and her peace of mind as they moved through the crowds.

This mood of sympathy suddenly changed. As she walked close to the colonel's side, she was forced to change direction when he suddenly took a slight turn to the left. Trying to see ahead at whatever made the colonel change directions, she could only see the crowd. She immediately realized he was more than a foot taller than her and could see over the heads of many; something had caught his attention.

A few steps further and she went on guard. A shop owner stood under the tent displaying his merchandise, and three men were arguing with him. They wore dark clothes and all had long black beards. One carried a rifle and another shook his fist at the shop owner. She knew they were FLN and perhaps radical terrorists.

She immediately knew there was trouble, and Colonel Devon

was heading right into it with a determined step. She knew his approach would not be peaceful. Undoing her sidearm holster flap and shifting her web belt and scabbard into a ready position, she moved ahead and slightly to his side. Sergeant Boivin also moved closer to the colonel and appeared ready.

"What's the trouble here?" the colonel asked loudly as he faced the men. He stood with his hand on his web belt, which held his service pistol, staring hard at them.

The men said nothing for a moment, only stared back at the colonel.

Finally, the one in front, obviously the leader, said in broken French, "We're just minding our business, soldier." He stood waiting for the colonel's reaction.

"Fine—if your business doesn't make trouble for the shop owners," the colonel said flatly. He stared at the leader for a moment. "If you don't want to buy something, move on."

The man gave a crooked smile and took a step forward, saying, "We don't have to obey the army anymore. Peace Treaty states that."

When the man stepped toward the colonel, Lieutenant Adelle took a step toward the man. She was poised, ready for action. Her look was focused on his face, and it was a harsh look.

The man laughed, saying, "Women soldiers belong in the mess hall." He continued his phony smile, leaning menacingly toward the lieutenant.

At that moment the one behind the leader touched him on the shoulder and mumbled something in Arabic. The leader dropped his smile and took a step back. He then said, "We'll leave but we'll be around." They turned and walked away.

The colonel smiled at Adelle. "Don't know what spooked them, but it was a good thing."

Boivin spoke up. "I clearly heard the one whispering; it sounded like the word *butterfly*."

CHAPTER 4

HELPING OUT

At the following morning meeting, Colonel Devon asked if anyone had any suggestion.

Lieutenant Adelle spoke up quickly. "Yes, I do." She waited a moment to get permission to speak and then said, "As more and more people decide to leave, they come to the docks and que up at the back of the waiting crowds. They're frightened and confused with all that's going on. I'd like to organize some in small groups to take charge and to move in the crowds around them to offer encouragement—and if needed, food and water."

"Not a bad idea, Lieutenant," Colonel Devon said. "Any idea how we can accomplish that?"

"Well, because of the nature of the work, I think the people will cooperate better if the female soldiers do the organizing. Male soldiers might make the women uncomfortable."

"OK, we'll stand in the background as you all work."

Arriving at the dock, Adelle went to work immediately. She approached a lady carrying a suitcase and had no children with her. She explains they might have to stand in line for a day or more before shipping out. This standing around for a time was more a hardship for parents with children. Could she help out by helping these ladies with children and getting others to help as well?. And she requested the lady and those helping her offer encouragement to all.

"Of course," the lady replied. "I lost my husband in the war and couldn't help out then. I'd be glad to help now any way I can." She went to work then, approaching a man and wife who had just walked up. After talking to them for a few minutes, she approached anther couple. She was soon giving instructions to a small group around her.

Adelle felt good with this first encounter and moved to another lady standing alone. She responded the same as the first lady, and now Adelle had two groups organized. The people were scared and uncomfortable, and a chance to do something worthwhile boosted their confidence and cheered them. With this, Adelle thought this was going to be easier than expected.

Colonel Devon and Boivin stood close by, talking encouragement to some who looked lost. They glanced back at Adelle as she worked, amazed at her effective efforts in getting her tasks done. They were used to seeing her in a strict military setting, and this new image impressed and inspired them.

The colonel had given much thought to how the army could best help the dislocated people. Obviously, they first needed food and water, but that wasn't all they needed. They had been forced to abandon their home and livelihoods. Many families had lived in Algiers several generations. Now they were ripped from their neighborhoods and homes and headed to the European continent with no means of finding shelter or making a living there. He felt the most they could do was encourage them and provide protection from radical elements of the FLN who were unpredictable and dangerous. Some of the Pieds-Noirs—people of French and other European descent who were born in Algeria during the period of French rule—were armed, but not enough to protect all. The army was needed. If not for the army, the radicals would mercilessly prey on the helpless people.

Colonel Devon was determined to do his best to help them. He instructed his detachment to mingle, saying, "We're here to help and protect you while you're waiting; It'll be better in France. People there will also help you."

There was no guarantee of these promises, but the colonel knew it was best for all, soldiers and citizens, to have hope.

Moving through the crowds, Adelle came upon a shaken older lady standing next to another lady who was helping her. They looked lost and frightened, and Adelle stopped to comfort them. She found out they were French sisters who were born in Algiers, and the younger one was caring for the other. Adelle asks if they needed water or food.

The younger woman said in a weak voice, "We have a few supplies. Save what you have for those who need it more."

Adelle was stopped in her tracks with a new realization of their evacuation efforts. It might be a day or so before these two could board the ship, and it looked like it might rain. How could they make it through the night standing in line?

Shocked, her mind searched for ways to give help to these two and others like them. "You ladies can sit down here. I'll find someone to stand next to you to keep others away."

"Oh, thank you!" the younger lady said and helped the older one into a sitting position.

Adelle left. Just a short distance later she came upon two young men standing in the crowd. She approached them and said with a voice of authority, "There are two ladies that need your help. Please follow me."

The men followed, and with Adelle explaining their situation, they offered to stand close to them to push the crowds back. Adelle moved on to help the next ones, and that's when the idea hit her like a thunder boom. She turned and walked quickly back to the colonel.

"Sir," she began with concern, "there's a situation we haven't addressed that needs attention. And it's serious."

Hearing Adelle's explanation, the colonel agreed they should do something but didn't know what could be done.

Adelle explained her idea and the colonel again agreed. He not only agreed but thought, *This is something I should have thought of.* "Any ideas what can be done, Adelle?"

"Yes, please follow me to the ship's loading ramp," she began. She then explained her idea to the colonel as they walked through the crowd.

At the loading ramp stood a captain and two soldiers. Adelle approached the captain, saluted, and told him of their special situation, making her request. The colonel and Sergeant Boivin just behind her.

An officer and sergeant, two heavily armed soldiers backing up Lieutenant Adelle, forced the captain's attention. He listened to Adelle's explanation, shaking his head as if he was listening to her request, and then turned to Colonel Devon. They talked for a while, and then the captain saluted and turned back to his men at the loading ramp, telling them of this new situation.

As the three solders walked away, the colonel wore a smile. With a chuckle, he said, "OK, Lieutenant, this is your show; lead on. We're behind you."

Adelle approached the two ladies sitting with the two men standing protectively close and asked them to follow her. She took them to the captain at the loading ramp. "Here's the first two, Captain. There'll be a few more."

The captain ordered his two soldiers to help the old people in line up the ramp. Adelle then returned to the beginning of the waiting people to search for others who needed help. It didn't take long for her to find all that needed preboarding and get them to the captain at the ramp.

At the end of day, the colonel was so elated with Adelle's performance he again offered to buy dinner for all. Sergeant Boivin begged of, saying he had some important personal work and needed to leave early. With the colonel's permission he left. No sooner was he gone than the colonel asked Adelle to join him.

The colonel congratulated Adelle as soon as she set at his table. Adelle was quiet, on guard as before, but she did want to talk about today's work; she felt good about what she had accomplished. "Thank you, Colonel. I feel we've done a good thing today."

"It was all your doing, Lieutenant. And I can't say how much I appreciate your work."

"Just my job. The people need our help, Colonel."

"And we do what we can," he said. "But now let's relax and let down a little and have a glass of wine."

Adelle said nothing. She was keenly aware of his close attention toward her.

The wine came and the colonel said, "Cheers to good work."

They drank to the toast. His eyes never left Adelle's.

She felt the look, and emotions stirred within her. She fought against the feelings, looking down at her glass.

"I'd like to bring up what we talked about the last time we had wine together," he said.

Adelle remained silent.

"You know how I feel about you," he said, not taking his eyes off her.

Adelle wished she were somewhere else. Her brow wrinkled and her voice broke a little as she looked at the colonel, saying, "Please stop. We're in the military. It's against the rules. I don't want to hear that."

CHAPTER 5

THE FRIENDLY ALGERIANS

Colonel Devon had been concerned with the morale of his detachment for some time. When he held a staff meeting and his office was crowded with personnel, he didn't see the playful pushing or hear the joking around his people usually did. They appeared uninspired about what was about to happen in the meeting. They knew that some new assignments would be ordered, and normally that caused them to be a little excited. But lately they just sat quietly waiting.

Looking for ways to inspire his staff, he thought of a celebration. As the calendar approached Bastille Day, he saw a chance to organize a company party in hopes of boosting morale. He wanted a stage, where a band could perform and a few awards could be given, plus a few benches before the stage. To set this up, he intended to use the army's civilian contractors who were on call when needed.

To the south of the army's installation was a community of Algerians who were friendly to the army. There were a dozen families here whose main source of income came from work they did for the army, such as building and street maintenance, waiters in the local cafés, and various other labor the army wanted. They were a sound community. They had their own school, their own temple, and a local government.

The colonel's order for the work came just before he got some bad news.

The Paris government was negotiating a Pease treaty with the FLN. And one FLN demand was the army was to disarm the *Harkis*, the nickname for the Algerian communities that had supported the army in the war. Orders came down from the war department in Paris to disarm the Harkis, including this community. Although the FLN soldiers at the normal discipline level would probably leave them alone, he knew the radical element considered them traitors and would attack. The radicals were uncontrollable, operated on their own mind-set, and were war-minded. They wanted to keep fighting, and no peace treaty would stop them. To take the Harkis's arms would leave these communities helpless to defend themselves from these radicals.

The colonel read the Paris order at his morning meeting and received many disagreeable grunts and frowns. He paused a moment, thinking. He said, "I'll not disarm our Harkis community. To do so would invite the radicals to attack."

The soldiers at the meeting gave loud, agreeable grunts.

"But you're inviting trouble from the Paris War Office if you don't do as they say," Lieutenant Adelle said with a worried look. She knew that when word got back to the Paris War Department, they would be upset and planning a serious reprimand for the colonel. This was one aspect of her bodyguard role she couldn't do much about.

"So be it!" the colonel said. "Our Harkis community has helped us, and I will not abandon them."

Members of the meeting nodded their agreement.

"Do we continue with our plans for a company party?" Sergeant Boivin asked.

"Of course," the colonel answered. "Now let's get on with our assignments."

Colonel Devon held a meeting with the leaders of the Harkis community, telling them Paris had ordered they be disarmed and to collect their weapons. They were shocked by this, for they had always been allied with the army. Devon told them he had been deeply concerned with this Paris order but finally had come to a decision—he would not take their arms. He asked them to keep them out of sight as much as possible, but if threatened, they should defend themselves.

The Harkis constructed a viewing stand in short order. It stood about four feet high and was broad enough to accommodate the entire band. A portable podium was brought out for the colonel to stand at as he handed out a few awards and congratulated his company on working well.

When the band started playing, the noise level from the soldiers crowded before the stage rose with excited talk and song. Some males asked the few female soldiers to dance, and they push the crowd back to give them room. The Harkis watched from a distance, proud of their part in preparation for the event and somewhat amused at the soldiers having fun.

The ceremony went well. It was nearing time to shut down when a gunshot was heard coming across the field from the Harkis community. The sound was faint, so far away to be barely heard. The army didn't take notice, but the Harkis standing on the outskirts of the army post heard and turned immediately, heading to their homes. When they got to their community, they found several women standing in front of their homes holding their husbands' long guns.

The wife of the Harkis leader spoke first. "Several men came and demanded we turn over our supplies. They said we were traitors and didn't deserve our stock of food." She stood firm holding the rifle at the ready. "I refused and when he started toward me, I fired over his head. He stopped but kept saying we were traitors."

"Did they touch any of our people?"

"No, they turned and went back the way they came. But as they left, they shouted they'd be back."

"It's the spinoff radicals. FLN can't control them." The Harkis leader looked around, checking to be sure all his people were OK. "I'll speak to the colonel about this. He's already said we must defend ourselves. For now, we'll assign someone so they can't catch us by surprise."

CHAPTER 6

FIRST WARNING

The day after the party, the colonel's team went back to working the docks. At the end of the third day, when his team reported back at his office, unexpected people were waiting in his office.

As he approached, his desk sergeant saw him and quickly moved to meet him. The sergeant motioned for him to step back into the hall. He was a little excited and hurriedly followed the colonel's team, saying, "Sir, there are two officers waiting who say they're from the Paris War Office. They insist on meeting with you."

"So?"

"I don't like them, sir. They're demanding and rude. They arrived about noon and insisted I call you back to your office, immediately. I told them you were doing some important work at the port. But they said, 'So what? Call him back here now; we want a meeting.' They're only captains, sir, and quite young. Isn't that an affront to your rank and office, sending two captains for a meeting?"

"Huh … the Paris War Office. Those officers who work closely with the politicians become politicians themselves. I've never like them either."

"I gave each of them a chair in your office to wait. One flopped down and propped his feet upon your desk. If he wasn't an officer, I would've clobbered him."

"Yeah, good call, Sarge," the colonel said with a knowing smile. "Those clowns in Paris think they're running the war. I'd like to see any of them face a terrorist who's coming at him with a ten-inch knife blade in one hand and a pistol in the other."

"I knew you didn't want to be called back for these idiots, so I told them there are thousands of people waiting at the port and it may be hard to find you. When they appeared angry, I told them I'd send out a runner, and left the room."

Colonel Devon dismissed his sergeant with a "good Job" salute and entered his office.

One of the officers stood while the other remained seated, showing disrespect. The standing officer introduced himself and the one sitting. Both were captains and were dress in class As that were immaculately pressed and neat. The colonel thought they looked too young to be captains in the army. *Got their rank with political influence,* he thought. *But they're just messenger boys.*

After looking them over, the colonel took charge. Towering over the one sitting, he snapped, "It's customary to stand when the commander enters his office."

He gave the one sitting a hard stare; the moon stood up quickly.

"Sir, I'm Captain Alain, and this is Captain Louis. We're here to bring a message from the Paris office."

"So what's the word from our fearless leaders?"

"Our office has received complaints through channels that your detachment has prevented the FLN from conducting their business. Specifically, you haven't disarmed the Harkis in your area. The Peace Treaty states there will no interference from the army. Paris is concerned with your actions."

The colonel smiled at the captain with a slight downward turn. He still wore his field gear: fatigues with heavy black boots, sidearm and web belts with heavy loaded clips, and a pair of binoculars strapped to his chest.

"Ha!" the colonel said with a hard look. "What's to keep the FLN from interfering with our business?"

"The Peace Treaty states you are to stand down with no conflicting business with the FLN," the captain repeated. It was obvious the young captain was uncomfortable passing a message to a colonel.

"Very well, Captain, you've delivered your message. Now, if you'll excuse me, I'd like to get out of my field gear."

He paused a moment and then spoke loudly to the desk sergeant. "Sergeant, will you show these gentlemen out?" He nodded back at the men as he removed his sidearm and web equipment.

"Sir, the War Office wants you to know they are with you in your mission and will be glad to offer advice on how to accomplish it."

Ha, the colonel thought. *How can they offer helpful advice sitting in a chair in Paris?* "Thank you," was all he said and turned away.

The two left immediately.

Colonel Devon hollered for the sergeant to come in and help him out of his "business suit."

His sarcasm went over well with the sergeant. He laughed, saying, "Glad you sent them on their way, sir."

"Yeah, but that's not the end of this situation. They were sent as a warning from Paris. They're watching me, afraid I'll complicate their negotiations, which I do not want to do. Whatever can be done to end this senseless war is a good thing. I'm under the command of the War Office and want to cooperate as much as possible, but at the same time I'll not abandon the people who have helped us. If we take their weapons, it will invite the FLN radicals to attack them. I won't stand for that."

'What about the OAS, sir? Where do they stand on this issue?" (The OAS was the *Organisation Armée Secrète,* a far-right secret dissident French paramilitary organization).

"I'm not sure about them. They're also war-minded, and I feel they will do whatever they can to keep the war going and keep the army here."

CHAPTER 7

THE YOUNG CAPTAINS

The two War Office captains wondered out into the street with nowhere to go. It was several hours before they could catch the Gooney Bird—the DC 3—back to Paris. Their mission of giving a warning message to the colonel in a polite way was accomplished. They stood before the army's street blockade, wondering what to do to kill some time. Their short time in the army had been confined to Paris, and they were excited to be in the war country. They wanted to look around in order to have something to talk about when they returned. They thought it would be exciting to have a brief confrontation with members of the FLN to have something to brag about back in the Paris War Office.

The soldier guarding the street was close by, and they knew they could get some information from him.

"Hey, Sergeant, where can we find some interesting cafés to check out?" Captain Alain asked.

"Check what out?" the guard asked.

"Some kind of action."

"What kind of action? You looking for women?"

"Oh, no. Don't have time for that," Captain Alain said, laughing. "Well, to be more specific, where do the FLN hang out?"

The soldier looked suspiciously at him. "Why do you want to know that? The FLN is our enemy and want to kick the French out of Algiers."

"We're officers in the French army, Sergeant, and we know what we're doing. We just want to talk to some ordinary FLN supporters, not the war-like ones."

"If you insist on knowing, there are cafés down in the Muslim section that cater to the FLN, but I advise you to stay away from them." The two captains left the soldier shaking his head in disbelief.

They moved down the street, hoping to find something interesting. They visited cafés, but nothing interesting happened.

"Well, we got that done; it didn't take much time." Captain Alain said. "I'm disappointed they didn't show more respect for two officers from the War Office."

"Same here," Captain Louis said. "They could at least have offered us a meal."

"Yeah, and I'm hungry, and we don't catch the Gooney Bird back to Paris for several hours. We can kill some time. Let's find a café and get a beer and sandwich."

"OK, but let's do some sightseeing while we're here in this war-torn country. How about checking one of those cafés the sergeant mentioned down in the Muslim section? If we run into FLN we'll have something to tell when we get back to Paris."

The taxi driver looked at them questionably when they told him to take them down to the Muslim section where the FLN might be. He noticed how young they were and the fact they were unarmed. He told them it would not be a good place for unarmed soldiers to go. But when they insisted, saying the French army could go anywhere, he took them to a café where he knew the FLN hung out.

When the two soldiers walked into the café, the normal chatter ceased immediately. Everyone stared at them in disbelief. The two ordered beers and waited patiently. The waiter didn't come immediately with the beers. He talked with other people in the kitchen for a while as they peered out at the two soldiers, discussing the situation. Although the customers were not the radical FLN members, they were nevertheless FLN sympathizers. Obviously, they noticed the men were unarmed and ignorant of the situation.

Finally, two waiters came out of the kitchen carrying large open containers of beer and approached the table. They both seemed to stumble, dumping the beer across the table onto the two captains, splashing across their uniforms, soaking them with beer stains

The captains jumped up, wiping away the beer, ready to fight. But when they looked around, they saw several men had stood up and faced them. The captains approached the outside door and found several men blocking their way.

Meanwhile, the taxi driver knew something was wrong and decided to report it to the colonel's office.

When the colonel learned what happened, he sent Lieutenant Adelle and Sargent Boivin down to rescue them. They were heavily armed. In addition to carrying their sidearms, they carried MAS 64 submachine guns. They didn't expect to be challenged but being heavily armed helped ensure that.

"Stand clear of the door," Captain Alain ordered in his best command voice.

The men did not move.

"You're holding up two French soldiers," he continued.

The men looked at them in a menacing way.

He moved to push past them, but they shoved him back.

"You're not supposed to be here," one of the men said. "Now that you're here, you'll do as we say."

The two captains pushed toward the door but were shoved back viciously. They stood not knowing what to do as they faced the men.

At that moment the door opened and two soldiers appeared.

They were heavily armed with large pistols on their sides and heavy ammo belts around their waists. Each carried a MAS 64 submachine gun and stood in a ready position.

Lieutenant Adelle and Sergeant Boivin stood ready for anything. The colonel cautioned that the Muslims there were FLN but not the radical terrorists, and planned to get the two idiot captains out without a fuss.

As the two stood in the doorway, the word *butterfly* could be heard whispered around the room. Lieutenant Adelle was well known for her skill with the handgun. And they knew that being a female, she would not confront any of the men in a physical way because she would be overpowered. But they knew also because of this weakness, she would use her handgun and that would be the end of anyone confronting her.

"You soldiers get out of here, now," Lieutenant Adelle commanded. "Wait for us down the street."

The lieutenant and sergeant stood in the doorway while the captains fled the café and rushed down the street. The café crowd stood back watching the heavily armed lieutenant and sergeant, who stood firmly and looked capable of much action. They all knew not to face the butterfly lady, for she could bring down three men before they got their weapons out. After the Paris soldiers cleared the area, the lieutenant and sergeant calmly walked away and joined the captains.

"OK, captains," Lieutenant Adelle began, "the colonel has commanded us to escort you to the airport where you can wait for the Gooney Bird. He also commands you not to leave the area before the plane arrives."

"But Lieutenant, we can't go back to Paris with our uniforms in such a mess. How can we get our uniforms laundered before we go?"

"Not enough time. You'll have to go back as you are."

"But we'll be seriously reprimanded with uniforms like this."

Adelle thought for a moment. "Here's how you handle this. You say you came to a war zone and inadvertently got into a fight with the FLN. You put them on the road but in the scuffle, you uniforms got messed up. You might even put a scratch on your face to look like you were in a fight. You'll be heroes."

Both captains said nothing, but they were smiling. They could imagine themselves facings their friends and the War Office as heroes.

CHAPTER 8

MAHAD

In addition to helping those at the ports, the intelligent detachment had to worry about the OAS, which was growing stronger and becoming a threat. At the Monday morning meeting, the colonel said he wasn't sending all his staff to the ports today and wanted to consider this situation. He addressed this, saying they had ignored the OAS situation long enough, and it was time to face that crisis. He went on to say he had some ideas but had not worked a direct approach yet. He dismissed the staff.

"Lieutenant Adelle, stay in place, please. I've got an assignment for you."

"But sir, I've already got an assignment from the general, and that's to stay close to you, the same as Sergeant Boivin." She immediately went on guard, thinking he may want to get personal again.

"What I've got for you can be done along with the general's assignment," he said, watching her closely. He paused a moment, and then turned to Sergeant Boivin, who had remained in his chair. "Sergeant, will you step out into the outer office a moment and wait there? Tell the desk sergeant to fix you a cup of coffee. I have some instructions for Lieutenant Adelle that's best done in private."

"Of course, sir," the sergeant said as he stood. He was used to assignments where he stood and walked about doing assignments and bored with the duty to stay close to the colonel. He was obviously glad to get away for a short time.

The colonel then turned back to Adelle, saying, "Lieutenant, we've got some problems new to our detachment. It's a strange and sad situation where our own army is beginning to break up."

He paused a moment to take a pull from his cigarette, brow wrinkled, leaving his face worried. When he spoke, he looked at her with concern. "I think you know what I'm talking about."

"Are you referring to the OAS, sir?"

"Exactly! And it is difficult to be planning something against our own. But I've received information they will go after us if we disagree with them. Some of them are as radical as the FLN radicals."

"Yeah—as if we didn't have enough problems dealing with the FLN terrorists, we now have to watch those in our own army who have rebelled against Paris. If you're in trouble with Paris, maybe they'll side with you."

"Maybe, but we must know what they're up to."

"Can't we just ignore them, sir? They're not that big."

"But they're growing rapidly. This miserable war has hardened some so much they won't stop fighting."

"Can't we let them continue their fight without worrying about them or confronting them?"

"Not anymore. They've became so radical they insist the rest of the army join their cause and threaten harm to those who don't."

"Umm … that's serious, our own army threatening its own."

"Yes, how disappointing is that? But it's a fact, and we can't ignore that, and we must know what they're planning." He paused a moment and then continued. "I've learned they're actively approaching soldiers from our own detachment to join them. I'm confident personnel in the intelligent section will not."

He paused again, looking closely at the lieutenant. "But we

must know, per General Chalet's orders. We need someone who's supposedly with them to keep us informed, and I have a plan."

Spy *on our own people,* Adelle thought with disbelief. *My God, I hope he's not going to order me to do that. I would hate to have to do that.*

"But sir, I know of no one who could side with them and report to us," she said, hoping to disengage herself from that possibility.

"Well, I have someone in mind, and I want your help in getting this organized." The colonel waited then, as if giving Adelle a chance to offer something. When she didn't answer, he continued. "I think a good person to get into their organization would be Mahad."

"Mahad!" Adelle exclaimed with surprise. "But sir, Mahad has done so much, and he's still working with the FLN. That's very dangerous, and if we continue to use him as a spy, he's surely going to end up badly."

"He's the perfect one to infiltrate the OAS."

"But he's just a boy, sir." Adelle was frantically searching her mind for an argument that might change the colonel's intentions about Mahad. She had already planned to bring him in to the port work, knowing he would fit right in helping out. "Isn't there someone else who could do that work?"

"I know, and I understand your concern," the colonel began with sympathy. "You brought him in and helped train him and have a strong concern for his welfare. But he's one of us and would be perfect for this assignment."

"But are we asking too much for someone so young?" She stared at the colonel with pleading eyes. She knew that someone operating as a mole had a strong chance of being discovered, and that would be the end of him.

The intelligent detachment had lost someone in that situation the previous year and she remembered him well. This person was a highly intelligent and experienced soldier yet was discovered by the FLN. With that in mind, Adelle knew Mahad could not survive indefinitely.

With a worried mind, she spoke up, seriously nodding for emphasis. "Sir, I volunteer for that assignment and let Mahad stay out of it."

"Won't work, Lieutenant. You're as popular as a movie star, too well known as command security, and they know it and won't trust you." The colonel looked at Adelle with sympathy, as if he understood her concern. "Besides, you already have an assignment per the general."

"Isn't there someone else we could send? Someone with experience in such matters and someone who might better avoid being discovered?"

"No one as good as Mahad," the colonel said, regret in his voice. "We'll get him back and protect him as soon as we learn what they're up to."

Lieutenant Adelle remained quiet. She wanted very much to prevent Mahad mixing with the OAS.

"Now, what I've planned for you is to be his point of contact. You can do this along with the security duty."

Adelle didn't speak for a moment, but when she did, she said angrily, "If anyone harms him, I'm going after them!"

It was obvious what she meant. She couldn't stand up to a large soldier in hand-to-hand fighting, but if confronted would not hesitate to bring him down with a bullet.

While plans were being made for Mahad's new assignment, he was busy in special training that the command had decided could be useful. Although he had no formal education, it turned out he was highly intelligent and was suspected by his instructors of having a photographic memory. He picked up languages quickly, and as soon as command learned that they put him to work further learning French. An interpreter that knew the various Arabic dialects and could instantly convert their conversations to French was a valuable asset. He could converse with Muslims in their language and repeat the conversation in French, something only a few soldiers could do. The command even decided to throw some German at him because the army was recruiting from that country. Not only was he useful as an interpreter, but because of his youth and nonthreatening appearance, he could enter organizations without creating suspicion and was the reason the colonel planned to use him to get inside the OAS.

As important as his training was to the army, it was important to Mahad, as well. He loved the learning and the attention he got, and this made him feel important, something he had never experienced before.

Mahad didn't blink when told what his new assignment would be. Not mature enough to fully realize the danger, he was excited to be brought further into the detachment's work. He was briefly trained and told the assignment would be dangerous. But that didn't worry him. They also directed him where many of the OAS soldiers hung out. It was a café and bar that catered to the ideas of the OAS, because they knew they couldn't exist if peace was declared and the army moved out. He was instructed to simply wander into the bar as if he was a street kid and appeal for a handout. Then, if they let him hang around, he could appear disinterested but listen to the chatter. If he heard anything that he thought important to report back to the detachment's analyst, he would report it, and they would get it to the colonel.

At the café, Mahad found it crowded with soldiers drinking and laughing at each other's stories. Some stood at the bar hovered over their drinks and glancing around occasionally to speak to someone at their elbows.

A couple at a table in the center of the room were arm wrestling, grimacing as they strained their muscles. A third soldier also sat at the table and was encouraging them on while two more stood by.

One spoke up, "I'll take the winner!"

"No! I've already spoke for the winner," the other one standing said and gave his partner a playful shove. It was a café catering to off-duty soldiers drinking and relaxing.

Mahad stood for a moment in the doorway, dressed in filthy gray trousers and a dirty white shirt with a tear on one shoulder. He wore a grimy-looking gray hat that was now so dirty the word on the bib but was indistinguishable. He appeared very much a street kid and was comfortable in his disguise, allowing him to be to be at ease in the company of the soldiers.

"Hey, no street kids in here!" one of the managers said as he walked up to Mahad.

"But sir, can't I just stand here out of the hot sun for a moment?" Mahad was very polite and bowed slightly. "And can you give me a glass of cool water? I've been out in the sun all day, and I'm so thirsty."

The café manager looked at Mahad with sympathy. "OK, kid, stand over there out of the doorway and I'll get you some water. But you can't stay long."

Mahad moved to stand against the wall between two tables. Each table has soldiers occupying them, and they were in heated conversation. They only glanced at Mahad as he stood against the wall. Mahad only looked down as if totally disinterest in any of the activity.

"There's only one way to get Paris to notice us," one soldier was saying. He spoke as if angry. "And that's the same way the FLN does it—create problems they can't ignore."

The other soldiers listened closely.

"Any ideas on that?" one asked.

"Yeah, I'm thinking of blowing up the city library," he said, looking around as if for support. "It's not used much since Paris began proposing a peace treaty."

"But that'll get the regular army on us," another soldier said. "And Colonel Devon's detachment will be hard to handle. I don't want to go against them."

"I know, and he's siding with Paris."

"Then he needs to go!"

"Wow! You're suggesting we eliminate the colonel. That's pretty extreme. And that'll not be easy. If they know you're coming after him, those bodyguards will be ready. I don't want to go up against them. Those two are the best."

"We have no choice. He's in our way."

Mahad was listening to this conversation with fear. It was unheard of to assassinate their colonel. He felt like standing and fighting the whole OAS group singlehandedly. But he knew he couldn't and that this was important information to bring back.

He left the café immediately, and bypassed the analyst to report directly to Lieutenant Adelle, who he knew would know what to do.

Adelle gave him a "good work!" compliment and instructed him to stay in quarters for a time. She then went to the colonel with the information.

She begged him to take this information seriously, saying," This is a new threat, and a big one. The sergeant and I will do all we can, but there are gaps in our security we can't cover. I suggest you stay away from other soldiers until we know who we can trust. And that means stay away from the docks. You're too vulnerable there."

"Ha!" the colonel exclaimed. "I'm not going to let those rebels scare me. I'll face them. With you and Sergeant Boivin covering my back, I'll go up against them. I'm looking forward to that."

Adelle was worried; she felt she had excited his fighting spirit when she wanted to appeal to his intelligence and make him more careful. But she knew once the colonel got going, there was no stopping him. She decided she and the sergeant would have to watch not only for terrorists but some of their own soldiers, as well.

CHAPTER 9

THE CAFÉ

Soon after Mahad reported the OAS was after the colonel, a situation developed that put them more on guard. At the colonel's morning meeting, he shared that the FLN had plans to attack their spy café in the Muslim district. This café was set up for normal business for all seeking a meal and catered to mostly by Muslims. But it was in fact a French army café operated by Captain Naafi, a Muslim captain in the French army. It had been used for some time to gather information on suspected radicals who often visited the café. Somehow the FLN had learned of its true purpose. And in spite of the peace treaty, they were out to destroy it and those associated with it.

The colonel shared that some of his detachment was pulling away from helping at the ports for a time to provide security at the café. Some of the army's people worked the café to gather information and thus must be protected.

He said, "The Paris government, when negotiating the Peace Treaty, agreed that our army would not interfere with FLN actions, but that is hogwash. We will take care of our own in spite of the Paris Agreement."

He paused a moment, looking around at his staff. A few grunts of agreement were heard. He continued, "I'm setting up extra security at the café. I'm already in trouble with those politicians in Paris, so I'm going to give them something to fuss at me about." He paused again, looking about the room.

"What more can you do, Colonel?" Lieutenant Adelle asked with a frown. She was anxious for some action but hoped for the best. To her dismay, her feelings for the colonel were getting stronger, causing her more worry.

"Well, here's what I'm going to do," he began seriously. "Working the ports evacuation our people had made me realize I can help more by getting out and into the middle of things. I've sat at this desk too much lately, and I need some action. I'm going to be part of the extra security." This caused the entire staff to mumble in disagreement. The colonel only smiled.

"But sir, if you're there, Sergeant Boivin and I will also have to be there," Adelle said. "We're still under the general's orders. Besides, the FLN would love to get you in a situation where they could go after you."

"Exactly why I'm going to leak it out I'll be in the café tomorrow for lunch. That'll surely draw them out at that time, and it's to our advantage to know exactly when they'll attack."

"A sure plan but a risky one for you, Colonel," Sergeant Boivin said. "Is it worth the risk to just get back at Paris?"

"I'm already on their hit list. Why not?"

The colonel's extra security was set up, and all involved reported to the café in early morning. The café was crowded. All inside tables plus the two street tables were occupied with numerous customers, eating or waiting to be served. Even the tables out back had customers drinking coffee or eating lunch. A couple of tourists stood just outside waiting for a table and chattering among themselves, while glancing down the street, as if thinking of looking for a less crowed café. Even Captain Naafi was taking orders and passing them on to the kitchen. Lieutenant Adelle's table was stationed to one side of the colonel's and Sergeant Boivin's at the other side. Their dedicated purpose was to provide security for the colonel. Not only was the FLN radicals a sure threat, with the colonel out in the open, there were unknown threats from unknown people inside the café.

The crowd was mostly friendly Muslim. Ramadan has just passed, and with it the days of doing without as the Quran required on this monthlong religious holiday with five daily prayers and no eating from sunup to sunset. Now they could celebrate by getting back to normal with meals and mixing socially. It was a friendly gathering with a chorus of conversations and occasional loud laughter. Tables and chairs were situated around the main room as usual. One exception was a small table with a single chair placed near the front entrance. Here sat a large individual sipping coffee, looking inconspicuous. Unknown to everyone in the café except the colonel's people, this individual was an army member in disguise who the colonel had added for extra security. Certain information had come to the army analyst, and putting this information with others, it was suggested the FLN had knowledge the Muslim owner was in reality a captain in the French army. If true, this was a serious situation for the army, and especially for Captain Naafi, the supposed owner. For when the radical elements of the FLN discovered someone was a spy and working against them, they would go after them, and they had a special way to assassinate these individuals. They held off shooting them; instead, several terrorists viciously attacked with long knives, leaving them cut up and dying. They did this to show the assassination was a special one for traitors to their cause.

Army intelligence was certain the FLN knew the Muslim Café was an army café for gathering information. The colonel had set up an ambush for the attackers who were sure to come. He was there as bait. He kept Lieutenant Adelle and Sergeant Boivin with him, and they were situated at tables to either side of his table. In addition to the colonel and his people was a sergeant in disguise by the door. He appeared as a normal customer sitting by himself. The extra security was well needed. Some other listening shops, spread around the city, had been discovered by the FLN radicals. When this happened, they viciously attacked the occupants and burned their shops. This café was an important asset for the army as was Captain Naafi. He would be a target if an attack came. Even though concerned, the colonel thought his added security could handle most situations that might develop.

Both the captain and Lieutenant Adelle were well aware of this situation and were always alert. Captain Naafi kept his service weapon, an 11-millimeter automatic, under a hand towel just inside the kitchen door. It was too big to wear since he only wore a light pullover shirt as he worked. The colonel had them all stay in uniform with their issued sidearms and not the small Berretta.

Lieutenant Adelle was prepared mentally, as usual. She had previously been in shootouts with terrorist, and it usually didn't end too well for them. She was a member of an international shooting club representing the army and had won many shooting contests. Normally she had the Berretta because it was small and was more comfortable under her shirt. But the colonel's orders had her switched to the heavier MAC 50, which had more firepower, with nine rounds in the magazine.

The café and the colonel's team had been on alert all morning, the café becoming very busy with nothing happening. They had drunk many cups of coffee and were now having lunch. They had become somewhat lax.

It was just after the lunch hour was well underway and most everyone had been served. Adelle was having a cheese sandwich with lettuce and tomato and a cup of tea. She had just taken her first bite, and it went well with her hunger. She was enjoying the sandwich because she had not had breakfast. A second bite was just started when a booming blast exploded at the front door, and she stumbled backward by the concussion and debris.

She knew immediately what had happened. The radical FLM

members had started using grenades when they were to attack someplace they knew was defended. They would throw in a grenade and then enter, shooting. She knew two of their listening locations that had been confronted this way, and the owners were brutally attacked.

The concussion and blast debris hit her soundly, forcing her down, her food and drink blown across the room. She hit the floor for a moment but recovered quickly, knowing the radicals would be charging in with guns firing. Her military senses immediately became alive; she drew her sidearm and pointed it at the front door, expecting FLN to charge in while shooting wildly. She was sure she could bring two of them down as they entered, and stood with her firearm cocked and ready. But no one entered the café. Without taking her attention from the front door, she glanced around the café.

The area around the front door was heavily damaged, a white smoke hanging in the air. The soldier sitting there had been blown back and now lay on the floor, face down and moaning.

She had a brief thought to go to him and see if she could help, but the colonel shouted, "Take cover, there'll be more!" as he crouched, pulling his weapon.

Lieutenant Adelle didn't move, standing in a ready stance with her gun pointed toward the door. She knew if anyone wanted entered, she'd bring them down so fast they wouldn't have time to look around. But no one entered!

When it was apparent that there would be no follow up to the grenade explosion, the colonel shouted, "We need ambulances immediately!" He then hurried to the fallen soldiers. Several calls were made and the caller begged them hurry; they had injured and bleeding people. When the all-clear was announced, most in the restaurant moved to help the wounded.

After helping with the injured, Colonel Devon stopped, looked around, and swore loudly. "The FLN has outsmart us again. But our day is coming, and I don't care what the Peace Treaty says."

CHAPTER 10

BACK AT THE DOCKS

After the conflict at the Muslim Café, Colonel Devon gave those who were there a day off. He took his day off to visit each soldier in the hospital. The soldier that was nearest the door had some serious injuries to his head and upper body but was strong and healthy. The doctors said he would recover in time.

He had the standard comment when the colonel asks him how it was going. "It's going OK, Colonel, but would have been better if I'd ducked."

At the following morning's meeting, the colonel announced, "That plan didn't go so well, but we saved the café and, more than likely, Captain Naafi. I'm keeping extra security posted. We had planned our line of security starting inside the café. That wasn't enough. Now I'm setting that security line to begin in the street before the café."

He was quiet for a moment, taking a draw from his cigarette and exhaling the smoke, coughing once as he looked around at the staff. He then asks if there were questions.

"Yes, sir," Lieutenant Adelle said. "Can we get back to helping those shipping out at the docks? There are still thousands waiting and they need our help. And I think it's a good idea to take Mahad with us. He could help by encouraging the folks, and maybe identify the OAS soldiers he heard talking in the bar if they show up."

She also wanted to keep Mahad busy to lessen his chance of being assigned to another dangerous project. And she couldn't forget all those worried and strained faces she had witnessed at the docks. She wanted to help and struggled mentally to come up with more ways. She was thinking that what the colonel's outfit was doing was not nearly what an army could and should do.

"Absolutely, Lieutenant! We'll continue our tours through the crowds, encouraging them, and stay on the lookout for anyone who might give them trouble. I've noticed at times some soldiers there who I didn't think were our people. We want to weed them out at every opportunity. I won't hesitate to ignore that Paris Treaty and go after radicals who bother our people."

"Yes, we need to do more, Colonel. It's bad enough they're having to abandon their homes, friends and neighborhoods to face this. Some are passing out in the heat."

The colonel looked worried as he looked around at the crowds.

"I'll think of something," Adelle said. "I've got to think of something," she repeated. "Our people are suffering! They're not only suffering here, but when they get to Europe, many can't find a good place to live or find jobs. The Paris government is trying to help, but there's only so much they can do. They can't handle so many immigrants."

When the detachment got back to the docks, the usual crowd was there. More of the Europeans were deciding that Algiers would not be a safe place to live with the FLN in control. It wasn't only that the FLN would try to control the populace. The normal Muslim people would act civilized, but they couldn't control the radicals; they were a vicious and unpredictable lot. And without the army, the Europeans would be hounded and threatened constantly. With this knowledge, more and more Europeans and a few Muslims were showing up at the ports wanting to get out.

The day was scorching, as North African regions often get. And the people were crowded together close to the landings, hoping to get in line for loading. The temperature within the mass of people was not only burning hot from the sun but from the jam-packed bodies pushing against the pressure of the crowds behind them as they tried to get closer to the loading ramps.

Lieutenant Adelle felt the suffocating heat as well, causing her deep concern. "Something must be done," she mumbled to herself. "This situation would tax the strength even of army personnel if jammed together. Even on bivouac while in the field it's not this bad."

As that thought struck her, an elderly woman collapsed in front of her, and several people stooped to help. With her shock from this scene, an idea came to her, and she turned quickly to the colonel.

"Sir, I know how we can help with this situation!" She spoke anxiously, causing the colonel to look her way.

"Name it, Lieutenant. Your ideas are always good."

"Well, we have our field equipment at supply," she said with urgency. "Why, just a mess tent would shield many from the heat, and we have other tents and are experts at setting them up. I suggest we set them up here to protect our people."

The supply sergeant stood close by. "We've been ordered to ship our field equipment back to Paris."

The colonel spoke up quickly. "To hell with that order; it can wait." He turned to Adelle. "Lieutenant, you're absolute right. I'm already in trouble with Paris anyway. This will show them where we stand with this treaty of theirs."

He turned and addressed a soldier, telling him to go to supply and requisition the field tents.

"And bring the water barrels as well!" Lieutenant Adelle hollered as he hurried away.

The colonel smiled down at Adelle. "Your ideas keep us going,

Lieutenant. Good work!" He then took a step closer so no one else could hear and spoke softly. "You're always in my thoughts, you know."

Adelle, turning away, said nothing. But a certain warmth spread throughout her as she walked to stand a few steps away from the colonel, obviously avoiding further conversation with him. She chastised herself for giving in to her feelings, telling herself to calm down.

It wasn't long before a five-ton truck pulled slowly up to the crowds. Several soldiers jumped out and started to unload tents and water barrels. They were experienced in setting up field equipment, and it didn't take them long to have the tents and water barrels set up. They immediately set up the cots and pulled down the tent flaps on the sun-facing side, then begin helping the disabled inside.

"Sir, you know we're in trouble with Paris holding up this shipment to them," the supply sergeant said. "They said they were going to ship it to Haiti."

Lieutenant Adelle said, "We need it more than Haiti. And we'll need it until all our people don't need it."

She and other soldiers helped direct and organize the loading of the people into the tents. Adelle insisted the sick, elderly, and women with children find their place first. She stayed focused on helping the people, but in spite of fighting it, she still had the warmth of the colonel's compliment within her. It irritated her, knowing she was having trouble ignoring the colonel's attention.

Mahad stayed busy helping. He wore his fatigues and army cap and brown army shirt with the pullover ARMY sign. He didn't wear a sidearm. Being unarmed, Adelle though Mahad would relate to the people better and they could relax with him. He would guide the elderly to a spot in the tents set up for them, then pass out water and food while encouraging them. After showing a man who was helping a woman who had fainted find a place to lie down for a while, he thought of more ways they could help.

He approached Lieutenant Adelle. "Lieutenant, ma'am, there's more we can help with now that we're using army equipment," he exclaimed.

"What's that, Mahad?"

"Well, a couple have passed out, and we're just lying them on the ground in protected areas."

"Best we can do."

"What if we brought out a few more cots to give them a place to rest?"

Adelle paused a moment. "Good idea. Why didn't I think of that?" She then went to the colonel and ask for permission to requisition several cots.

"Carry on, Lieutenant. It's your show."

"It's really Mahad's show, sir. It's his idea."

"OK, have him set up a few cots and be in charge of the area," the colonel said, while turning away from a soldier to whom he was issuing orders.

Mahad got the cots and set them up in a certain spot under the tents. He then went through the crowds asking if there was a doctor present. Finally, he found a doctor who would stand by in the area to help when needed.

Mahad continued helping, watching for anyone who fainted or seemed sick.

CHAPTER 11

ADELLE'S PROBLEM

It was Saturday, and the early morning sun was streaming through the window of Lieutenant Adelle's room, warming the area as she and Jennie sipped of coffee and made idle conversation.

A knock came at the door and Adelle answered it. A private held out a letter, saying, "Special delivery for you, Lieutenant. Just came."

Adelle thanked the private and took the letter back to the table where Jennie was sipping her coffee. As soon as she opened it, she dropped her head on the table, saying, "Oh no!"

"What's up?" Jennie asked, looking closely at Adelle. "Bad news?"

I don't know if it's bad or good," Adelle said, dropping the letter without finishing it. "It's from the colonel, and I know what he wants."

"Well, what does he want?"

"He wants to get together tonight for dinner and talk, and I can't."

"Yeah, I know he likes you very much, and just dinner would be OK, wouldn't it?"

"No. When we're alone he talks too personal. I don't like that."

"Aww ... you should be able to handle that."

"Normally, yeah! but there's something else going on. I'm beginning to like what he says, and it bothers me. I don't want a relationship with him. The army frowns on having a relationship with your commanding officer, and I know what the other soldiers will think. I'm up for captain, and this will look like I used sex to get promoted. I feel I'm highly respected now and don't want to affect that. I just wish I didn't have feelings for him. It's just complicating my life."

"But you have a right to certain privacies. Besides, you and the sergeant have a mission to watch after him. And it's a psychological fact that when you care for something, you become attached to that something. It could be clothes, pets, whatever—and especially in your situation with the colonel, it's a person."

"Well, I just wish I didn't have this problem. I've worked for years to gain my reputation and don't want to ruin it. It's something very important to me and I don't want to lose that."

"You do have a problem. But hold out for now. You're close to the end of your enlistment, and when that happens, you can be on your own with a free mind. Also remember that old saying: to get over one, get another."

CHAPTER 12

THE RESCUE

During the peace negotiation, much was overlooked and ignored. The Paris negotiators didn't concern themselves with Muslims who helped the French and tried to bring about peace. One such person was a Muslim named Mahdi, a moderate who the FLN considered an enemy and had placed him and family under house arrest. He had a wife and six-year-old son. Because he had worked with Paris, he was well known to the Paris government, and it was also known he and his family would be mistreated after the army left the country. Plans were quickly formed to send a rescue team to bring them to Paris for their safety. Several methods were considered, and much consideration was given to avoid any conflict with the ongoing negotiations. To have the remaining army get them would violate the treaty terms already formed, and no one wanted that. After many approaches were considered, it was decided the safest way would be to send a small team and have them study the situation close up to find a way to bring about the rescue without too much commotion.

An officer, Captain Louis, who worked with the War Office was selected to go, because he was highly intelligent and had combat experience. And because he was so highly respected, he was offered the option to select a teammate to make the trip with him.

Lieutenant Adelle had known the captain for some time and had even had dinner with him on several occasions. She had enjoyed his company each time. He was polite and entertaining, and she rejected his attempts to sleep with her

Because of his easygoing approach, she was relaxed with his attention. And knowing his history and reputation, she had a strong respect for him. She had even considered taking Lieutenant Jennie's advice—that the best way to get over somebody was to find another to replace him. The idea stayed with her; it was a way she might get over her feelings for the colonel, which was giving her much anxiety trying to forget.

Adelle knew of the project and hinted to the captain she might be interested in going. It worked, and when the captain was asked who he wanted to take with him, he selected Adelle. He said since it was a family they were going to aid; it would be a good idea to have a female to help with the care of them. This was true, but in reality, the captain had grown fond of Adelle and wanted her close. This, plus Lieutenant Adelle's reputation as the Butterfly Lady might keep the FLN away.

Adelle had been bored with her job and was looking for something interesting to do. She readily agreed to make the trip, thinking with the close contact she might grow fonder of the captain, which would keep her from thinking of the colonel. She simply had to get over him.

Adelle was assigned as the captain's partner to make the trip and help bring about the rescue. Not knowing what opposition they might encounter, they carried not only their sidearms but the MAS 38s as well. Their contact in Algiers said the FLN had a soldier who stood close to the family to keep them under guard, and if they worked quietly, this would be the most difficult problem they would face. Before they left, they were also warned not to miss the return Gooney Bird flight in the evening because the daily schedule of the plane was being cancelled. Sadly, after the Gooney Bird had served the army so well for so long, it was being put on standby. On the trip down to Algiers, Adelle sat close to the captain, shoulders touching, because the flight was crowded. She enjoyed this slight contact, thinking she would encourage more of the same. The captain seemed to feel the same.

At the captain's request, the War Department had arranged for them to have a three-quarter-ton truck, a vehicle large enough to accommodate all in getting them to the Gooney Bird at the airport. The captain also asked for two of the airport soldiers to follow close behind with their submachine guns. The captain was technically minded when dealing with military matters, and he explained the best way to avoid conflict was to show overwhelming force, which would discourage confrontations. Adelle agreed with this tactic and was impressed with the captain's knowledge and skill in dealing with possible hostile situation.

Once on the ground, Adelle's attitude became serious, aware of the conflict they may encounter. She drove the three-ton truck, with the airport soldiers following close behind in the lead jeep. They studied the surroundings as they passed the address where the family lived. Outside the house, a jeep sat with a member of the FLN, keeping the family guarded. Observing the FLN member, it appeared he was somewhat older and had relaxed with nothing to do and dozed off.

They pulled up to the jeep and got out, waking the guard. They saw he didn't have a radio so he couldn't call for help. Adelle relaxed, thinking they didn't need such a powerful force to confront the single guard.

But she felt responsible, and, approaching him, he didn't seem aggressive. "We're here to relocate the family," she said. "We have orders."

"But you're the French army, and it's the FLN that has

responsibility," he said with concern. "I have had no orders that the army was taking over."

"Well, sir, as I said, we have orders and will carry them out. if you just sit quietly"—Adelle began politely— "we'll collect the family and move on with our orders."

"And if you don't resist, we won't harm you," the captain said, looking hard at the confused soldier. The captain and Adelle had moved their MAS 38s from their shoulders to their hands, and the FLN soldier looked from them to the airport soldiers that supported them and offered no resistance.

"But I'd be ignoring my assignment."

"Just stay quiet and you'll be all right." the captain warned the confused man.

Adelle went immediately into the house to get the family organized to leave. She explained their mission was to get them out of the country. "One small suitcase only," she said. "And you must hurry."

The family was relieved that someone was coming to their aid and quickly threw a few items in sacks and bags and loaded up in the truck. The captain drove them straight to the airport. The FLN member was left standing confused, but he was not going to challenge two French soldiers with submachine guns.

Adelle had observed the actions of the captain as he took command and was impressed. Her feelings for him had grown since they left Paris, and she welcomed those feelings, thinking, *This will help me get over the colonel. It's just what I need,* but something stirred in her conscious she didn't understand.

At the airport a number of French soldiers were stationed to guard the Gooney Bird while it waited for its passengers. The captain took command, ordering the soldiers to spread out and watch for trouble. The FLN might attack to get the family back.

He got the family loaded, then picked a location at the back of the plane for him and Adelle. It was a crowded plane, and he and

Adelle were forced together. With the Goony Bird reached its flying altitude, she whispered to him, "How about dinner tonight?"

"For sure, and it's my turn to buy."

They reached Paris, and the family was happy to be safe and out of the war-torn country. They were set up with the War Department authorities, who placed them in a secure location in the city. As the soldiers parted, the family thanked them profusely with handshakes and hugs. They also received congratulations from the War Department, and each received an extra three-day pass for rescuing the family with no major conflicts.

That evening at the dinner with the captain, Adelle felt good about the assignment and about the captain. She had grown closer to him while on the assignment and welcomed her feeling's, thinking, *OK, colonel, I've finally found a way to get over you.*

For several days, Adelle kept the captain on her mind. He seemed to show up when she and Lieutenant Jennie decided to catch a meal at the cafés. The rest of her day was spent shadowing the colonel as ordered. But even then, she recalled the way the captain looked at her and the way their eyes locked. The attraction was real, and she begin to imagine being in bed with him. He suggested they get a hotel room each time they got together, but Adelle always laughed it off, saying something like, "Why, Captain, we have just met!" or, "It's late and I need to get back to my quarters."

He would return a laugh, saying, "OK, but don't blame me for trying." He was so easygoing and casual with his request that Adelle was relaxed with him. She thought seriously about sleeping with him, thinking that act would help distract her from emotional thoughts of the colonel. But that was a big step. She was always so strictly military-minded that she suppressed her emotions and had never slept with anyone before. He would be her first. It was not the way she had always dreamed it to be, but she was getting desperate, afraid she would give in to the colonel. And to do that would destroy her reputation as a career soldier. She knew nothing else, and that reputation was important to her. She was determined not to lose that status.

She worried about the sleep-together situation so much, she finally had to talk to Lieutenant Jennie about it. She laughed, saying she had a boyfriend and slept with him regularly, and that it was quite pleasant. Adelle still wasn't sure; she was just too proud of her reputation as a career soldier who always presented a straight-backed military image and never let a man get close to her emotionally.

She cautioned herself, though, that her main duty was to protect the colonel, and that was an order from the general. Under no circumstances would she ignore her orders, but she thought she could handle both situations. But when the colonel was out in public and she was watching every situation around him, when her eyes weren't on him but scanning the area around him, she continued to feel close to him emotionally.

Finally, she made up her mind; she would sleep with Captain Louis in hopes this would keep her emotions away from the colonel.

After dinner, she suggested they have an extra glass of champagne and dance a little after the meal. When it was time to retire, the captain, as usual, suggest they get a hotel room.

She surprised him with a little laugh and said, "Why, Captain, I thought you'd never ask!"

He was elated, and with a smile, said, "Let me get a special bottle of champagne and then find us a nice room."

The captain hailed a taxi and directed it to a seaside hotel in the north of the city. He had obviously been there before because he asked for a special room with a view of the blue waters of the Mediterranean. The champagne went quickly, leaving both relaxed and feeling pleasant. They made love with the mild ocean breeze drifting in through the open windows, cooling their naked bodies. Since it was Adelle's first time it was a strange experience, but the closeness and the obvious need of the captain gave her a pleasant time. In reliving the details the following day, she had to admit it was a good one, but one thing left her annoyed and angry: several times during the evening, an image of the colonel popped into her head.

CHAPTER 13

ADELLE'S PLAN

Colonel Devon was constantly worried about the people at the ports. His command had always been concerned with protecting the Algerian Europeans, and now that they were being forced from their homes, he was even more determined to help them. As they queued up at the ports, he went every day to do what he could to provide a little hope and cheer. Of course, Lieutenant Adelle and Sergeant Boivin closely followed him around, watching every move he made and the activity around him.

Adelle missed Captain Louis and wished he worked in Algeria so she could see him more often. She was afraid that if she didn't have frequent contact with him, the colonel's attention would overcome her resistance. With no other distraction, Colonel Devon's constant care and praise of her work and ideas might cause her to give in. She missed the distraction the captain provided and wanted him transferred to the colonel's detachment. She struggled with different ideas that might convince the colonel to have him reassigned to his command. She knew she had to be careful, that if the colonel suspected he had competition with Adelle's attention, there would be no way he would bring the captain aboard. She finally came up with an idea after seeing one of the young soldiers that carried himself well and was strikingly dressed and displayed several medals. He was impressive and his appearance had people admiring him as he moved through the crowds, cheering those he met. He was an asset to the army's cause.

The idea came to her that Captain Louis would be a good person to help that way. He stood out impressively when dressed in class As and displaying his many medals, since he was a decorated war hero. And to add to his credit, he could be outgoing and friendly to those around him when he wanted to be. The more she thought of it, the more she wanted to get the captain involved in the port work. She knew it would be a strange request for the colonel if she requested him to transfer the captain to his command. She struggled with this problem, looking for a viable reason to have him working with them. Finally, one night she woke with an idea that might work: to have a famous war hero mingling with them as they wait would cheer them and help them brace up.

After much thought, the lieutenant decided she would do what she could do to get him transferred to the colonel's command. She began while walking with the colonel in the crowds and passing the sharply dressed soldier she had previous admired. She pointed out the soldier to the colonel, saying, "Sir, have you noticed how effective that soldier is at greeting the citizens? They seemed to cheer up somewhat when he meets them."

Umm ..." the colonel responded.

"I've watched him as he moves through the crowds offering conversation. He's a French soldier, and the people seem to relax more when he's around. The people look up to him."

"He is impressive. Wish we had more like him."

"Sir, with your permission, I could look around for more like him."

"OK, give it some though, Lieutenant. Good job."

"Thank you, sir," Adelle said, while thinking, *Well, I've got the first step going. I'll be careful and search for the next step.*

Adelle spent some time trying to come up with a reason to bring Sergeant Louis to the colonel's command. It would seem odd to bring a single soldier down from the Paris War Department when they considered the colonel had sufficient personnel already. And it could only happen if the colonel requested he be reassigned to his command.

With the war slowing down, there was a surplus of personnel in Paris, so it could be done if the colonel requested it. She couldn't come up with a clear plan but was determined to work on it.

Her break came when the colonel was making his way through the waiting crowd, and the sharp-looking young shoulder happened to be in the same area. She left the colonel's side and approached the soldier. Taking note of new stripes being pinned to his arm band, she knew he must have recently been promoted from private to corporal.

"Corporal, come with me," she commanded, walking up to him.

"Yes, Lieutenant," the soldier said, turning away from a couple he was talking to. He was surprised but did what an officer ordered him to do.

She led him before the colonel. "Sir, this is the soldier I mentioned to you. He's recently been promoted, and I thought it proper you notice him." The colonel had previously asked Adelle to point out things he might miss.

Lieutenant Adelle commanded, "Attention, Corporal!"

The man snapped to attention, displaying a sharp, professional look.

"Congratulations, soldier," the colonel said, looking him over. Obviously, he was impressed. "At ease." Then, "How long in the army?"

"Three years, sir!"

"Good work; you've done well." The colonel paused a moment." Back to your duties."

The soldier saluted the colonel and walked away. He approached a couple with a child and began talking to them, obviously to offer encouragement, complying with the standard order.

Adelle viewed this with approval. As she looked on, a plan came to her. Whenever possible, and without being obvious, she pointed out the soldier to the colonel to see him in action. This would be her big chance to bring up Sergeant Louis as an excellent candidate for this duty. She had her plan and hoped, over time, it might work.

Twice in the next three days, her plan was carried out. Both times, as the colonel's group approach the sharp looking soldier, he was talking to a group of citizens as they crowded around him. The crowd obviously wanted to hear what the sharp soldier said and moved in closer. He was telling them the army was close by and would not allow any of the radicals to approach. He further mentioned that a team of workers would be waiting when they arrived in France to guide them and suggested places to go from there.

Adelle casually pointed out to the colonel each time the soldier was at work and the positive effect he was having on the crowds. The colonel acknowledge each event and said, "Good man." But the third day when this happened, he said, "Good man; wish we had more like him."

Adelle knew it was time to bring up Sergeant Louis. "Sir, I don't know of anyone here that rises to the level of excellence this soldier does." She paused a moment for effect. "But I have worked with a sergeant who was just that excellent."

"Well, bring him around for me to see."

"I'm afraid that's not possible. He stationed with the War Department in Paris. I got to work with him on that assignment where we rescued the family the FLN was holding hostage. And I was impressed with his military image and sense of command in getting the job done."

"Umm …" the colonel said, still looking at the young man. "He seems to be cheering up that group around him. They're giving him their close attention."

"Oh, yessir. I've listened to his talks, and he's definitely encouraging them. We need more like him."

"Check around, Lieutenant. See if you can find more like him."

"Yessir," Adelle said, concealing her excitement. This could be her big break. She would casually work on bringing the sergeant down to the colonel's command.

She contacted Sergeant Louis in Paris, telling him how the people waiting on the boats felt isolated, lonely, and frightened. They were crowded at the docks waiting for the unknown and were scared the FLN radicals would come after them. She told him a soldier of his status and history could be a great comfort to them by mingling with them to protect and encourage them as they waited.

Sergeant Louis was immediately responsive, saying, "I want to help and will put in for a transfer, but I'll need help on your end as well."

"I'll be working on this end for the transfer," Adelle said. She was excited with the sergeant's response and started immediately making plans to influence the colonel. She knew what impressed him, and one of the main things he respected in another soldier was his military decorations. The sergeant had won Frances's highest medal, the Legion of Honor, and this fact would be Adelle's strongest argument.

The following day, at the morning's staff meeting, the colonel stated he had met a most impressive soldier the day before at the dock. He described the soldier and said he wished they had more like him and if anyone knew of someone like him, to bring it to his attention.

This was Adelle's chance to bring up her sergeant in Paris. "Sir, the sergeant I mentioned before would be a great asset here. He's always immaculate, as if on parade. And when he displays his medals on his uniform, it's really impressive. And he's got the Legion of Honor."

The colonel nodded, definitely interested. "Legion of Honor. Don't many have that. When can I see this soldier?"

"Well, that's the problem. He's stuck with the War Department in Paris. He wants to get out but has no support so far. I asked him if he would like to come down and serve in your command, and he gave a definite yes."

"Interesting. I'd like to check him out. Get me his War Department contact and I'll see what we can do to bring him down here."

"Yessir! Right away, sir!" Adelle was elated. Her plan was working. She would contact Sergeant Louis immediately to set up a phone meeting with the colonel.

CHAPTER 14

PROBLEM BREWING

After reviewing Captain Louis's military records, the colonel talked to him by phone. Satisfied with his research, he requested the War Department reassign the officer to his command. With no wars in place, the War Department had a surplus of personnel and readily granted the transfer.

A week later the captain arrived in Algiers, and the colonel put him to work at the docks. To Adelle's pleasure, he ordered her to show him their routines. Captain Louis adapted to the work well and was immediately helpful with the crowds. He would approach someone who looked fearful and lost and calmly encouraged and reassured them. Being an officer, he could also direct soldiers to tasks he thought important.

The FLN sent some members to mingle in the crowds, obviously to show they were taking over the country. But if any of them started something, a soldier, who was usually present, would step in. Adelle was quick to point out the way the people seemed to brace up as the captain walked through the crowds. He was "army," and the army was there to protect them. And at first his presence helped her not think about the colonel, but in time her feelings returned. This caused her to focus harder on Captain Louis and their lovemaking.

After a time, though, unexpected events developed. A conflict began between Sergeant Boivin and the new soldier. It was a natural development between two highly respect individuals where each was accustomed to getting lots of attention for their work. Now they both were aware of the other getting attention also. It started when the colonel was leaving for a meeting with the general. As he started for the door with Lieutenant Adelle and Sergeant Boivin close behind, Captain Louis happened to be in the office.

After inquiring from Adelle their destination, he turned to the colonel. "Permission to accompany the escort, Colonel. In the future I might have an assignment to visit the general's headquarters, and this could be my chance of knowing the way."

"Permission granted."

As the party headed out, Sergeant Boivin said quietly to Adelle, "We don't need this guy following us."

"I agree, but what can it hurt? Besides, he outranks us." Lieutenant Adelle felt the conflict growing. She thought, *We can't let this go on.* She cautioned herself to pay little attention to Captain Louis when Sergeant Boivin was close. This worked out OK for a while, but in time the captain noticed and complained to Adele. Now Adelle had to be extra careful and show disinterest in either when they were all together.

In spite of doing her best to quiet the tension between the two soldiers, they continued to find fault with the other's actions. It developed into a climax when Adelle and Boivin were off duty and having lunch at a café in the army's section and Captain Louis walked in. Seeing the two together, he walked over and sat uninvited at their table.

In spite of being outranked, Sergeant Boivin spoke up with obvious irritation, glaring at the captain. "Should be no secrets between us as we're all working on the same projects."

Captain Louis suppressed a smile, as if he knew he was out of line but didn't care.

"I'm going to say this just one time," Boivin said, his body tensing up. "Leave us be!"

"Now, boys, lets us be polite and get along," Adelle tried to head off the conflict.

"Meet you outside," the captain said, standing up.

"Yeah! It's time we settled things," Boivin said, also standing up. "Take off those captain bars, and I'll be glad to accommodate you."

"Oh no!" Adelle said, standing up, getting between the two. "The colonel won't like it if you boys fight."

She knew both were experts at fighting and someone was sure to get hurt. And if one showed up for an assignment with evidence of fighting, the colonel would know and would not like it. Soldiers sometimes went at it when they disagreed over something, but not the colonel's personal staff. Soldiers fighting each other were more likely to forget their assignments. He made it known that his personal staff members must act and perform in a professional manner.

Adelle was disappointed in both men, especially Captain Louis, who had conducted himself so well in his previous contact with the terrorists. It was the first time she found him disappointing.

CHAPTER 15

THE HARKIS

Working their way around the back of the crowd, the colonel's team scanned the people, looking for reasons to help.

Adelle spotted a man pushing and shoving a lady, who turned out to be his wife. Adelle calmly walked to them and asked the gentlemen what the problem was. She spoke softly, knowing the stress of leaving their homes and evacuating often caused problems within families.

"No problem, Lieutenant," the man said. "We just disagree on where we'll go once in France."

"Well, can you two be more polite in your disagreement? Calmly talk it out, please. That'll help you and those around you." Adelle's quiet manner helped them settle down.

Although Adelle was extremely polite when settling disputes, she was ready to use her authority, when necessary, to settle issues. Almost always, though, that was not necessary. For she was an imposing figure in her fatigues and boots, with sidearm and web belts holding the extra clips and the heavy belt up. Also, the colonel had them wear a cloth sign the said Army, which was a pullover item and lay across their chest. This extra identification was necessary because just soldiers in uniforms didn't prove they were members of the colonel's staff. No one resisted these soldiers.

As time passed and with fewer people crowding the docks, they moved further to the west, where a small village of Algerians who worked the ports lived. The people populating this area had always worked the ports and naturally worked closely with the French and other countries that had ships docking. They were called Harkis and worked closely with the army. Being supporters of the French, they were considered traitors by the FLN and hounded unmercifully by the radical element. They were beaten and often assassinated for no valid reason. To make matters worse, there was no protection for these people.

The Parisian politicians negotiating with the FLN were too willing to give in to their demands and ignore the Harkis. To the negotiators' shame, the army was even ordered to disarm them in an attempt to appease and negotiate with the FLN. This left them helpless to defend their families and community from those wanting to do them harm. The hardcore radicals murdered and robbed them frequently, saying they were traitors to their cause and deserved no pity. They were trapped between the hatred of the radicals and neglect of the Paris politicians.

However, the army at times disagreed with the Paris politicians, and some in the army remembered their assistance and were willing to help. Colonel Devon was one who had used their help occasionally and was willing to assist them.

As the colonel's detachment worked closer to this community, they observed a crowd of armed men surrounding a family. The family was huddled in the background and were obviously terrified. The armed ones wore the usual dark clothes, had long black beards, and looked dangerous. They were not FLN regulars but the radical element of the party, the war-driven men who were so obsessed with the war they wouldn't stop fighting. They were so driven they even attacked the milder members of the FLN if they didn't agree with them. Some regular members of the FLM suggested they excommunicate them for their violent actions.

The group of men had a man on his knees, before his family, and were threatening him with a long knife, their favorite way of dealing with those they considered traitors. The family was pleading with the men and the children were crying. One small boy ran at the man with the knife, trying to fight him. The man with the knife kicked him aside and then turned back to the man on his knees. His family were screaming, "Stop! Stop! Please stop!"

The colonel had stopped and was watching from some one hundred feet away at the edge of the crowd at the dock. He suddenly let out a cuss word, drew his sidearm, took quick aim, and fired one shot that caught the attacker in the head, slamming him to the ground.

With this action, both Lieutenant Adelle and Sergeant Boivin knew what was going to happen next as the mob of radicals turned their way. They moved to each side of the colonel, waiting to see what was coming. Captain Louis hung back. He seemed unsure of himself, glancing behind him obviously to see an escape route. The group of men brandished their knives and started their way. They were shouting, "Traitors! Die now!"

Lieutenant Adelle move one step in front of the colonel, and with a flash of her gun hand had her weapon out, and although a significant distance from the oncoming mob, fired from the hip several quick rounds. She was an expert at distance firing, and two of the men fell to the ground. Boivin and the colonel also had their weapons out and ready but were waiting until they came closer.

Captain Louis stood behind the colonel but had drawn his weapon. "There's too many for us to face," he shouted as he took another step backward. "We need to fall back and join up with the rest of our detachment."

He was openly concerned and obviously feared the situation. From a regular army training situation, he was right. The normal procedure when vastly outnumbered was to fall back to rejoin support groups or seek a good defensive location.

"I'm falling back to find our detachment," he said again and began to drift backward. He fell further and further from the colonel and his team, and Adelle took note.

She was surprised and disappointed with the captain's action. She was rapidly losing respect for him. She knew what the proper military position was in this situation, but her disappointment made her realize he would no longer help her escape from her feelings for the colonel. Certain situations called for special consideration aside from the military position. The captain had violated one of her strongest personal attitudes—that you do not abandon an associate, leaving them in danger. This action caused the captain to become history with Adelle. And with the captain no longer influencing her feelings, she was back in the situation where she had to constantly watch her moods and actions when around the colonel.

In spite of being in the open and facing the hostile mob, the colonel stood his ground, pistol ready, with Adelle and the sergeant standing with him. The radicals, as they moved toward the colonel, begin firing in their direction. They were an undisciplined lot with no training, and although dangerous, their shots were mostly over the colonel's team's head or into the ground.

Adelle felt a tug at her left shoulder, causing her to realize a round had just passed through her shirt. Another round nicked her shoulder but didn't penetrate her body, leaving only a scratch. Boivin took a round that nicked his leg, but he could still walk. The colonel was slightly behind Adelle and Boivin and did not receive any wounds.

Although the radicals' gun firing was mostly ineffective, the colonel's team was deadly accurate. When Lieutenant Adelle fired her weapon, she quickly picked out a spot on her target, and each time one of the men coming at them went down. After a few rounds, she reloaded a fresh clip in one quick movement and continued firing.

The colonel's team were highly trained and experienced in battle. They stood firm facing the oncoming men, returning deadly active fire. The battle lasted less than a few minutes, and the crowd rushing them suddenly were mostly out of ammunition except two who, seeing their friends falling like tilting dominos, turned and ran in the opposite direction.

"Don't shoot them," the colonel said quickly. "Let them carry this message back to their headquarters."

The colonel then went to the Harkis family who were tending to their wounded member. The man had only a slight knife cut in the muscle in the back of his neck. He seemed to be coming around with his treatment, and the colonel nodded, saying, "I wish we could help your people more but can't. You might consider moving to Europe along with the Pieds-Noirs and away from these war-mad people."

Returning to the dock crowd, the colonel glanced back at the Harkis family as they moved the wounded man inside. He knew the FLN radicals would be coming around again, especially after his team had shot up some of their members. He returned to the family before their home. He asked one member to go to the adjoining homes and request the occupants to come out where he could talk to them. There were only three other families living there and they congregated in front of their homes to hear what the colonel had to say.

"You folks are not safe here when the army leaves," he began. "The FLN radicals will be back as soon as we leave. I suggest you pack one suitcase and queue up with the Pieds-Noirs at the docks to go to France."

"But we're Algerians and this is our home," one woman said. "We've always lived here, raised our families here."

"I know, but the radicals think you're a traitor to their cause and will come back and do you harm."

"But how can we survive in France?"

"You must work to survive the same as the displaced Europeans will have to do. It will be hard on everybody, but at least you won't be hunted like animals."

"Where can we go in France?"

"Since you have been dockworkers here in this country, it's probably best you settle close to the ports in Europe. With your background, you'll find work there and should fit in."

All three families had gathered around the colonel as he talked. They were frightened and knew what he said was true. Talking among themselves, they agreed with the colonel, saying they would immediately prepare to queue up with the rest of the people at the port.

"Good," the colonel said. "And I'm assigning a soldier to stay with you until you've joined the crowd at the port."

As his team returned to the port, he said, "History will show the Paris Treaty a disgraceful neglect of their former ally!"

CHAPTER 16

SECOND WARNING

As days passed, the crowds gathering at the docks begin to thin. Thousands had already shipped out to Europe, and fewer new ones were showing up to be shipped out. Almost all the Europeans had left Algiers, as well as many of the native people, knowing what would happen as soon as the FLN took over. The FLN had some good people but many hate-filled radicals who would be looking to punish whoever they thought worked with the French. And, with the radicals, it was well know they would blame their victims without proof and punish them. Many innocents would be caught up in the vengeful action. It didn't matter if they were Algerians or Europeans. The situation for many staying in Algiers after the FLN takeover was not good.

After a slow day, the colonel announced they would leave early, have dinner, and then meet and discuss what they had accomplished and how they should proceed. He and the others felt good helping their people and took seriously their plans to continue.

Lieutenant Adelle especially was happy with her place in the team. She carried memories of picking up and holding crying children and drying their eyes as they quieted down. The army tents and water barrels were very helpful. She constantly moved around through the people looking for someone to help, and she had not seen anyone fainting or passing out since the tents were installed. Many in the crowds thanked her as she walked among them. And as usual, when alone at night and reliving the events of the day, she remained surprised at her changing disposition from a strict military one with a tough approach to one with deep sympathy for those needing help. She was slowly evolving from a firm military mind to that of a caring woman. But she hadn't forgotten that Captain Louis had abandoned them in the midst of action. With the demise of her feelings for the captain, her feelings for the colonel resurfaced and grew stronger.

When the colonel and his escorts approached the colonel's office, the desk sergeant met them out in the hallway, holding them up with both hands spread out, excitingly saying, "Colonel, there are some important people waiting in your office from Paris and they're very impatient. When they commanded me to send a runner to find you, I said I would immediately, but didn't, as you had instructed me. There's a general and two civilians and they're from the War Office."

"Very well, Sergeant," the colonel replied calmly. "I've been expecting such a visit." Turning to his security team, he continued. "You two take a break and wait for me in the outer office."

"Sorry, Colonel, our orders to stand beside you are from the general. We must obey these orders." Lieutenant Adelle spoke apologetically but faced him directedly.

"Oh. Well follow me. But you'll see something you don't want to see."

In the colonel's office they found a general fully dressed in class-As with medals, and two formally dressed civilians in white shirts and black ties. The three stood up as they entered and began talking at once. After all were introduced, the general apologized and announced they were from the War Office. The two civilians remained quiet, obviously rehearsed to let the general do the talking.

"Well, I'm glad to finally meet you, Colonel. My name's General Gains, and these two gentlemen are from the War Department and are members of the War Council. This one is Councilman Albert and the other is Councilman Simon."

The councilmen nodded with a slight bow, hands at their side, as was practiced in Paris.

"We've had a long plane ride and hope to get our business over and headed back home as soon as possible," Councilman Albert said.

The general spoke in command mode but was professional and polite. He was aware of the colonel's reputation and even revealed a little awe facing him. He had never been in war, himself, and was awed at those who had. "You know your detachment is quite famous in Paris. We're all proud of your accomplishments." He then turned to those with him. "Isn't that right?"

"Of course," came the immediate reply. The councilmen nodded.

He then turned to Adelle and Boivin, asking, "Who are these soldiers? Why are they here?"

"That's my security team."

"Security team! Why do you need a security team?"

"We're in a civil war, General. The terrorists are very active."

"Pardon me, sir," Lieutenant Adelle said. She was somewhat out of line but didn't seem to care. "Our analyst has learned the colonel is on their assassination list." She then stood back in respectful silence.

"I see!" the general said, looking at the lieutenant.

He studied her a moment and then asked, "Do you know how to use that sidearm? You're too pretty to be a soldier."

Without a flicker of facial expression change, Adelle let the general's attempt at complimenting her go but addressed the gun question. "I've been in the army eight years and have been in several conflicts. I'm also on the nation's firing team and hold the award for the most accurate firing both near and far. I hold the world's record for drawing and firing; my recorded firing time is .4 seconds."

Both the colonel and Boivin wore little smiles as the colonel spoke up. "She's had several face-to-face gun fights with terrorists, and it didn't end well for them at all. The terrorists all fear her and have a special name for her."

"Just what's is this special name?" the general asked with interest. "I'm sure it has to do with her stunting good looks."

"Her special name from the radicals is Butterfly."

"Really? Well, that must mean she is as beautiful as a butterfly."

"In our business it very complimentary. To them, it means stay away, because she's very fast and can shoot the eyes out of a butterfly!"

The general said nothing further, seemingly stunned at the description of Adelle. He just stared at the lieutenant in awe.

The silence lasted but a minute and then the colonel spoke up. "They're always with me when I'm out, General." The colonel paused a moment. "And what brings you here on this visit, may I ask?"

The general cleared his throat, pausing as if collecting his thoughts. Finally: "Colonel, Paris has been proud of the work you and your detachment has done fighting terrorism. I know you've lost some close ones in this war and we sympathize with you and your command." He paused a moment again. "But I've got some bad news. And personally, I disagree with Paris's decision. I'm a soldier like you and if in your situation would probably do the same thing."

"OK, shoot, General! I already suspect what this news is."

"Well, Paris has decided to relieve you of your command!" the general finally said. He spoke with a genuine sympathy.

The colonel only smiled a knowing smile. "I saw it coming but wouldn't change anything we've done."

One councilman spoke up then. "Colonel, Paris is afraid with your activity fighting the FLN you'll be detrimental to their attempts at negotiations with them. The final straw was that shootout your command had with the FLN a little while back. You wiped out a dozen of their members."

"They were attacking a family."

The councilman stared at the colonel for a moment. He looked at the general for instructions, and with a nod from the general he turned to the colonel to speak. He was obviously in a difficult position. Finally, he got his thoughts together and stammered, "Paris is relieving you of command of the intelligent detachment and putting you on retirement. You're to report to Paris as soon as possible."

The colonel only looked at the man a moment. "Twenty years serving my country and this."

The general said, "Such an unfortunate situation, Colonel. But it's not just you; they'll be pulling the army out and many will be discharged."

The colonel said nothing for a moment. When he spoke, it was with resignation and concern. "Let's just hope the politicians negotiating the treaty protect our people."

All was quiet for a moment.

The second councilman had not said much. But after a moment he shuffled around slightly as if he wanted to say something. Finally: "You three wiped out all those terrorists! How'd just the three of you do it?" He was obviously awed to be facing the colonel and his people and knowing what they did.

The colonel said, "We're in a war, and sometimes such things happen."

CHAPTER 17

SHUTTING DOWN

The following morning, when Lieutenant Adelle and Sergeant Boivin reported to the colonel's office, he was busy piling items on his desk.

"Security team reporting, sir," Lieutenant Adelle said.

"Good! You can help me get my stuff packed."

On the colonel's desk were several notebooks, a small box with his accommodations, several other personal items, plus a firearm, a US Army .45 that was awarded him for work he did with the United States concerning the Cold War. Although the colonel had the pistol for many years, it appeared well cleaned and shined like brand new. In the box were several medals, including the *Croix De Guerre*, a medal for bravery during battle. He had earned that one as a young lieutenant in a skirmish in Indochina and was most proud of it. He had a suitcase sitting beside his desk that was closed tightly.

"You're traveling light," Adelle said. She was unhappy about the affair, and it showed in her face. "It's not going to be the same without you. We'll certainly miss you."

"You're not going to miss me just yet. I've been ordered to bring you two along with me as I'm still a target." He glanced at the lieutenant as he fumbled with a pair of binoculars while inserting them into a well-worn case. "Had these since China."

The lieutenant looked at him with a pleased face. She maintained her look longer than necessary, as if she wanted him to know. With Captain Louis faded into the background, her feelings for the colonel resurfaced. "I'll stay with you with pleasure, Colonel. When do we leave?" She reached over and held the binocular case to help him put it away. With that accomplished, she stepped back.

"Tomorrow's evening Gooney Bird return. You two be ready." He paused a moment. "I'm told you two will be offered a discharge once in Paris."

He looked long at Adelle and then spoke with feeling. "I'm hoping we'll settle close once we're out of the army." His look stayed with her. He obviously felt strongly about her and didn't want to separate.

Adelle looked away, afraid to return his look. "Maybe. I'm thinking of getting out."

"Me too," Sergeant Boivin said with a smile. "It's been too long coming."

"Well, hopefully we can stay in touch after discharge," the colonel said. "I'm calling my staff in this afternoon to say goodbye."

They already know the army's pulling out," the lieutenant said. "Some are not happy about that."

"Yeah, my desk sergeant is one. He says all he knows is the army," the colonel said. "I've spoken to the general about him, and he says he thinks they can assign him to government security in Paris."

The following evening the three boarded the Gooney Bird for the last time.

CHAPTER 18

CIVILIAN LIFE

With the war over and the soldiers going home, Lauren, her close friend back in Heidelberg, was so happy the fighting had stopped that she wanted to celebrate. After discussing it with Mark, she had contacted Lieutenant Adelle before they left Algeria and asked her if she would organize the others and invite them to Heidelberg for a celebration. She emphasized she and Mark would arrange lodging and expenses for all. Mark was happy to please Lauren as their separation had made him grow even closer to her. He missed her and Little Mark greatly, and this was a worthy cause to get together. His construction company had performed greatly and they stood very well financially. He was a multimillionaire several times over, but work demands gave him little time to enjoy it. Here he would get to be with Lauren and little Mark and her friends, meet some of the soldiers, and he would be a hero, standing out as Lauren's husband and the benefactor of the affair.

Adelle was happy to be of help and extended Lauren's invitation to those she had been working with. She started with Colonel Devon; he tried to decline the invitation at first. She pleaded with him that those who had worked closely with him would be disappointed to split up with no fanfare.

The lieutenant's influence with the colonel had grown significantly in the past few months. They both had attraction for the other, but Adelle was holding off. She knew deep in her heart she loved him deeply but couldn't relax about the situation. Their feelings for each other happened long before they even knew it, but it continued to grow. But both, being so military minded, and not wanting to break the unwritten rule of no personal relations between commanding officers and staff, prevented a relationship. But her influence was strong, and with her persistence, he soon agreed. She then proceeded to invite Lieutenant Jeanne, Sergeant Boivin, and Mahad, along with a few others who had worked close to the colonel. All agreed despite some having doubts because they had jobs lined up after the army.

Mark flew in from New York early to help Lauren get ready for the celebration. He secured hotel reservations and suggested special plans for their house arrangement. He said he could move in with Lauren, leaving the spacious guest room available for someone special. This naturally turned out to be the colonel. They temporarily move Little Mark's bed into the room with Frau Lisa, allowing Adelle to have his room. When Mahad heard their plan to put him and Sergeant Boivin in a hotel, he objected, saying he didn't like hotels and pleaded to sleep on the floor of their front room. He had a sleeping bag and all the necessary items to sleep out in the woods, and the carpeted front room floor would be just great. Sergeant Boivin said that would work for him as well, because he was used to sleeping out on assignments. The other people from Algiers were happy to stay in a hotel.

When all were situated, they met at Lauren's and the celebration began. Much wine and cognac were consumed, and the celebration continued far into the night. Everyone laughed and told stories about their adventures with the army. But as time went on, the talk took on some sadness. Everyone knew they had failed. And not because they didn't do a good job but because of the FLN and other factions' determination to have independence. Paris had finally decided the cost of lives was just too great to continue the war. Toward the end of the celebration, when heads were woozy and everyone was getting tired, the talk turned to each other's plans for the future. Some had jobs line up and some were simply going back to their home locations.

The colonel had retired to his room without comment. But everyone knew he was retiring to the place where his wife and son lived.

Lieutenant Adelle said, "Well, the army has offered me a position at a training location here in France." She paused a moment. "I might try that for a while." The location of the assignment was not far from where the colonel was to live, and she spoke with pleasure.

Others spoke back and forth about their plans, but when Sergeant Boivin talked, everyone listened. "I've accepted a job down in South Africa."

"Really? What's down there?" Lieutenant Adelle asked. "Seems there's a lot of trouble between the tribes down there."

"Yeah, there is, and that's why I've been offered this job."

"Will you be safe down there?" Lauren asked.

"As safe as I was in Algiers." He stopped for a moment, as if considering what next to say. When he resumed, he seemed confident. "I've been offered a lot of money to come down."

"What kind of work?" Lieutenant Adelle asked. She had a serious look and seemed suspicious.

"It's the same as I've been doing," the sergeant said.

"In the South African army?" Adelle asked.

"No, with one of the warring tribes."

"As a mercenary!"

"Yes."

"Well, that's dangerous. Take care!" Adelle commented. She paused a moment with a serious look. "But it's your life."

"I'm leaving tomorrow," he continued. "And I'm taking Ahmad

with me. With his machine gun experience, he can bring a nice salary."

Lieutenant Adelle turned toward Ahmad. She saw he was obviously unaware of the sergeant's plan and looked confused and frightened. "Do you want this?" she asked him.

Ahmad said nothing but slightly shook his head.

Lieutenant Adelle turned back to the sergeant and said, "Ahmad stays here!"

"Who says?" the sergeant said, standing up, facing Lieutenant Adelle.

"I do!" Adelle snapped. She faced the sergeant.

"I'm not in the army now. Who are you to tell me what I can do?"

"Ahmad is just a boy. He doesn't need any more war." Adelle was poised as if she was wearing her sidearm. If she had been armed, the sergeant would have been more careful, for he knew well her capabilities. But even though she wasn't, she still appeared capable and determined.

Lauren spoke up then. "I'll find something for him. With his knowledge of Arabic and French, he can be a great help to our interpreters." She faced the sergeant angrily as well, and moved to stand by Adelle. Caitlan, her closes friend, also move to support Adelle.

The sergeant was a powerful man with combat experience and could be dangerous when aroused. He was determined to take Ahmad with him to South Africa in spite of Ahmad not showing any interest in going. Adelle and the other girls knew it would be a bad situation for Ahmad to become a mercenary and were determined to prevent that.

"You can't tell me what to do," Sergeant Boivin snapped. He made a move toward Adelle.

Mark stood up quickly, facing the sergeant. He said nothing, but it was obvious he was ready.

With everyone objecting to the sergeant, he stopped a moment, staring hard at the group, then turn and walk out briskly.

"He's been a good soldier," Adelle said. "But we can't let him make a mercenary out of Ahmad."

After the sergeant left, everyone relaxed and again discussed their plans for the future.

Mark stood up holding Lauren, with Little Mark beside him. "My future plans are to locate a secondary office here in Heidelberg. Between Abe and my general manager, Buck, they can run the company when I'm not available. I'm spending as much time as possible with my family, for everything I do is for them."

With a smile on her face, Lauren exclaimed, "Great! You can help with the housework!"

The colonel had returned to the room as Boivin walked out. He followed him outside where he,stopped him, saying, "Sergeant. you've been a good soldier, and I appreciate your help over the years and the security you've provided recently. But you've got three powerful women against taking Mahad with you. If you stop and think about it, I think you'll agree it's best to let Mahad stay here."

Boivin stopped and gazed out at the trees in the distance. Soon he turned back to the colonel. "I guess you're right. It's just that it's going to be lonely down there without some of my old friends."

"I understand. Since you're determine to go, give it a try. If you change your mind and want to come back where you have many friends, we'll find you something around here."

"What could an old soldier do here?"

"For one thing, I think you'd make an excellent policeman, and I'd vouch for you. And I would think you'd make chief in a short time."

Boivin said nothing for a moment, as if considering the colonel's statement. Then, "Thanks for everything, Colonel. I'm proud to have served in your command." He stiffened, gave a sharp salute, and then turned, walking away.

The colonel returned the salute and said, "Good luck, Sergeant!"

CHAPTER 19

A FINAL

After Mark and Lauren's goodbye party, the colonel took the train and returned to his new home. Because of the way the colonel and his intelligence detachment had defied Paris and continued to protect the Europeans and those Muslims allied with France, he was phased out of the army, bringing with him many commendations and medals. With his retirement he had moved to Vesoul, a village in east France not far from the German border. It was his family home, in the village where his wife was raised. He had kept the home after his wife and son were killed in a plane crash. The house had a back deck facing the west, and he often sat there with his evening cognac, watching the sunset and remembering.

After Lauren's farewell party he had said his goodbyes, giving much appreciation for those who had served with him. Sergeant Boivin had left earlier. The goodbyes were hard for him and he stiffened up as if in a command mode. It was especially hard to say goodbye to Lieutenant Adelle, who had gone with him to the train station. Just as the train arrived, he pulled her to him, his arms closely around her. He held her this way until he had to enter the train. When he pulled away, she clung to him a moment longer. His last words as he entered the train were, "I'm going miss you."

She had tears in her eyes. "I feel the same!"

In spite of army personnel cutbacks since peace in Algiers, they still needed certain sections to continue. Lieutenant Adelle was too important with military knowledge to let go. She was promoted to captain and given a training company to command. She did her best running the company. But command gave her little attention since the war ended in Algiers; there was little need for new recruits. She went through her days bored and hoping to hear from the colonel.

The colonel did write, telling her of how bored he was in retirement and casually mentioned he missed his old command and how he especially missed her. She returned his letters and also said she missed working for him. But touching base with letters never really expressed their real feelings.

Adelle fell into a bored routine of shuffling paperwork and going to the firing range for entertainment. She often got so bored she would get in her car and drive. She visited most of the battle sites, drove around Paris, and once drove all the way to Amsterdam and spent the night in a hotel. She had no reason for the driving but it seemed to help her feel better. She missed the colonel terribly but never expressed her feelings in her letters. She was too disciplined in military protocol to let him know, but her military mind was softening and she more and more thought like a woman. She played with the idea of visiting him in the future.

The colonel had his routine, as well. He was not someone who sat around doing nothing, knowing that inactivity would lead to low morale. In the morning after coffee and a light breakfast of wheat toast and blueberry jelly, he stripped down to loose-fitting, fatigue cutoffs and an army T-shirt and headed out for his morning run. Although he was tall with strong shoulders and arms, he knew he didn't look like a distinguish retired army officer, but he didn't care. Army life was in his past, they let him go and he let them go and moved on.

To improve his moods, he pushed himself to the extreme on each run, checking his time and trying to improve each run. When his loneliness got really bad, he upped his workouts by running a mile and then falling to the ground and doing pushups. He would do twenty pushups, rest, and then continue running. After his exercise and on his way home, he would stop at the local café and ravenously eat a breakfast of buttered croissants, several cups of coffee, a plate of bacon, several eggs, a pile of potatoes, and sliced tomatoes. Returning home, he would shower, get dressed in clean fatigues, and get to his day work.

His day routine was spent researching and working in war history. He worked untiredly, examining the war years and writing about them. He was especially concerned with terrorism and the inhuman act it was. To him, the killing of innocents for shock value took civilization back a thousand years. It was evil, and those that practiced it were also evil; they had no morality, couldn't be reasoned with, and he knew, as others, the only way to deal with them was to kill them. Also, he wanted to show how the nineteenth-century practice of colonialization eventually created war and failed in the end at horrendous cost to all involved. In spite of being a professional soldier, there was an anti-war theme through all his writings.

He kept himself busy until evening. After his evening chores, he would retire to his back deck, a structure he built himself. It faced the west, allowing him to watch the evening sun go down. With his cognac to lighten his moods and a usual slight evening breeze, he would let his mind drift back to his army days commanding his special intelligence detachment. In remembering some of his major decisions, he knew he had unintentionally made some unwise ones and readily admitted them to himself. But he was well aware that he had done his best, and most of his decisions were the right ones. His intelligent detachment had taken out many terrorists, saving many lives. In his mind he was successful at what he did, but he remained restless and lonely. There was something missing.

He often thought of the soldiers under his command and how dedicated and effective they were. His thoughts often dwelled on those he lost, remembering them with respect and honor. Losing Sergeant Leo Durant brought his greatest sadness. The sergeant's heroism was unsurpassed, and his accomplishments would always be remembered. He had gotten Aimu, the leader of the FLN radicals, taking out their most vicious terrorist. Losing him also caused his lover, Lieutenant Dugas, deep sorrow, forcing her to leave the army with battle fatigue.

But even with these memories his second cognac always brought his thoughts back to Lieutenant Adelle, and the loneliness would begin. He remembered how fresh and attractive she looked as she reported to work in the mornings. Even in her military uniform with sidearm, she still appeared feminine with a youthful face and smile that always brightened his day. And as the day went on how she became even more attractive to him.

He often fantasized about being alone with her at a quiet café, and over a glass of fine white wine telling her how much he thought of her and how he wished they could be together. Of course, with his personal sense of discipline, having a relationship with someone in his command was something he couldn't do. He sometimes felt she had the same feelings, for often their eyes would meet and stay focused on each other. He was now out of the army and no longer bound by the army rules, and he wished he had been more forward with Adelle.

After letting his thoughts go in this manner, he would get his third cognac and remind himself that he had missed his chance, thinking she had probably found someone new. They could never get together, and it was best to put those thoughts out of his mind. He often told himself, *I must give up hoping,* but he couldn't.

Sometimes when the seclusion and hopeless longing for Adelle got so bad, he let his thoughts go. There was an old army saying from many years prior: "Always save one bullet." The saying was to relieve the soldier in battle the angst of being captured and torture. At times, he reasoned he had nothing left to accomplish and nowhere to go with his life. The thought was so disturbing that he sometimes got relief from recalling "save one bullet," and it brought respite as it did to the soldiers in the old days. Once he even got his service pistol out and, placing it on the table before him, stared at it. Its lifeless, metallic form lay there as if a challenge. He looked at it a moment and then cursed himself for his thoughts. He put the weapon away and poured another cognac.

CHAPTER 20

COMING TOGETHER

It was midsummer, and the day was fading as he sat on his back deck, his feet propped up on the railing. Even on his third cognac his body remained stiff and tired from a hard workout. The cognac tasted good and helped to soothe the pain. The bottom of the sun was just touching the horizon, and the golden rays were bright and warm as they streamed through the oak trees before him. He had been especially down for the past few weeks and his drinking has increased proportionally. He knew that too much drinking would lead to problems, but he didn't care. Lately he had worked out more, trying to find diversion. But it was not working. He had just tilted his glass, draining the last bit there and was looking at the bottle on the stand next to his chair.

Suddenly, from the back of the deck, there came a voice, "Evening, Colonel!"

"Uh … what?" the colonel mumbled, turning to see who had spoken.

Adelle stood there calmly watching him. Not in uniform but dressed in a light gray dress and white blouse. The dress came above her knees a few inches, displaying shapely legs, and the white blouse fell off her shoulders, which added to her feminine look. Her hair was brushed back, displaying a youthful face with just a hint of smile. She looked feminine and very attractive.

"Lieutenant. I didn't hear you drive up." He stared, amazed at seeing her. It had been a while.

"It's *captain* now. I parked on the street." Adelle spoke quietly, as if giving him time to adjust to her unplanned visit and waiting for his response.

"You ... here," he stammered, the surprise clear on his face. "It's so good to see you!"

"For me as well."

"But why didn't you let me know you were coming?"

"I didn't know myself," she began quietly. "I was off duty this afternoon and just driving around after spending a sleepless night, worrying, and suddenly turned your way. It was unplanned."

"What's worrying you?" he asked with concern. "Whatever it is, maybe I can help."

Adelle remained quiet, just watching him.

"Please let me know how I can help," he continued, quickly standing, ignoring his cognac. "What's worrying you?"

Adelle finally spoke, disregarding his question. "Do you ever think of me?"

His answers came quickly. "All the time!" He then appeared surprised at the question, moving toward her a step. "All the time!"

"We've ignored things too long."

"What things? What are you saying, Adelle?"

"The army and all the ways they influence you with little concern for your personal feelings. They want you to think only about army things, like a machine."

"Well, the army is the army, and I'm out of it now."

"My tour is up soon, and then I'll be out of it. The army no longer holds me."

"But you're concerned about something, and I want to help."

Adelle stared at the colonel a moment before speaking. She

just stood there with a quiet look. "I've given my decision serious thought," she said in a determined voice. "We've waited long enough."

"Long enough?" he said. "What are you saying?"

Adelle didn't answer for a moment, just looking at the colonel, as if trying to think of what to say. Her gaze never wavered as they stood facing each other, both waiting.

Finally, with assurance and confidence in her voice, she said, "Move over, Colonel!"

"Why? What do you mean?"

"I'm moving in!"

Printed in the United States
by Baker & Taylor Publisher Services